LOVE BY CHANCE

Madhuri Tamse

INDIA • SINGAPORE • MALAYSIA

Dedication

I dedicate this book to all my readers who have loved Taani and Sameer, the side characters in my previous book "Mr and Mrs Kapoor." They definitely deserved a story of their own and hence I came up with the idea of having a separate novella for them – <u>Love By Chance.</u>

All my acknowledgements and dedications are incomplete without thanking my friend Kavita Wadnerkar (@kavitawadnerkar) who has always helped me structure the plots, and my editor, Sejal Shah Shrinivasan (@sejals_musings), who then uses her magic to polish my first draft into the final masterpiece. Thank you, girls. Love you for infinity!!

PROLOGUE

Taani

The kiss is pure perfection. My lips meet his as he runs his hands down my arms to my waist, gently caressing every inch of my skin until they reach my hips. Just the feeling of his hands on my body, holding me tightly to him while our mouths join to taste each other, is enough to make me feel desired and wanted. I've met numerous men in my business circle; many even showed an interest in me, but this man here is the only one I've ever wanted since I laid my eyes on him.

A tiny gasp escapes my lips as he removes his hand from my hips, but I take a relieved breath when he cups my face instead. I had no idea a casual dinner date with him would escalate this desire between us to such an extent that we would end up kissing each other in the confined space of the washroom of the Lake Palace Hotel in Udaipur, where we are staying for the past three days. The sound of our kisses fills the empty space while I lean against the grey countertop basin, with the weight of his body crushing me. My hands slide from his shoulders to touch his well-groomed French beard. It's a novel sensation for me, and I like it. It's prickly and a little rough, but I like the ticklish and heady feeling of it rubbing against my face. The beard gave him an edgy look with a boyish charm, and I always wondered what it would feel like to touch it, to feel it against my skin. When my nails stroke his beard, he lets out a moan and pushes our lower bodies together fervently. It feels more like a dream, a naughty one at that, bringing all my fantasies to life because the kind of woman I am, I would never ever let any man invade my private space so easily. But he is special. Ever since I saw him, he became special. My back arches greedily as our bodies meet, and I'm a squirming mess against his supremely male body.

I can already see the stars as his tongue dances seductively with mine making me a quivering mess. Good Lord, this man is a good kisser. Although I'd tried to find as much information about him as possible before meeting him tonight, I would never have found out what a great kisser he is if we hadn't indulged in our lips mating with each other tonight. My fingers tangle into his thick dark hair as he kisses me passionately, feasting on my lips and tongue, and the only thought at the back of my mind was that I don't want this to end. I never knew I had missed out on such amorous feelings in my life until tonight. I never knew I wanted this deep connection, this feeling of oneness with the man of my dreams, not until this very moment.

Man of my dreams?

These words instantly echo in my head on loop. He is not the man of my dreams, nor is he allowed to pursue me. This bitter realization dawns on me, and I push him away from my body. What the hell have I done? How could I kiss him? I think my brain got short-circuited with my hormones swirling around it. We both were a frenzied mess with unfulfilled, insatiable and uncontrollable need hanging between us from the time we met, which neither of us could ignore any longer.

I feel like I have committed a sin by allowing him to get close to me. He reads the anger and mortification on my face.

"Taani, I..." he tries to speak, coming towards me again, but I stop him right there.

"Don't even think of touching me again. This ... this shouldn't have happened, Sameer." I cover my mouth with my palm feeling appalled. How am I ever going to face him or my sister again?

"I know," he exhales in a rush, brushing his fingers through his messy hair. "This shouldn't have happened like this, but-"

I don't wait to hear his excuse and storm out of the washroom, banging the door loudly behind me.

How could I do this? Me and Sameer Khanna? Seriously? I was in Udaipur, away from my home in Delhi, for a business meeting. Then how did things heat up between Sameer and me to this extent that I lost all my control? His family had proposed his alliance for my younger sister, Vidhi. Though nothing is fixed, and Vidhi is yet to give her approval, how could Sameer and I cross this unspoken line between us?

He is forbidden. And after this act tonight, I'll make sure he doesn't even think about marrying my sister either. A man whose control could slip so easily despite knowing his marriage talks are going on with some other woman cannot be trusted. Ever!!!

CHAPTER 1

Sameer

The worst part about business conferences, like the one I am attending tonight, is that the speakers are really boring, and instead of adding value to your business, sometimes, they add value to your sleep. And yet, here I am, at the Hilton Hotel in Delhi, where the current conference is held. I came from London last week to handle a critical business deal, and Dad insisted that I attend this conference as he could not do so himself.

'Only for you, Dad,' I mutter before making my way to the Conference Hall. It is fully packed, and I grab a seat in the last row. There were many young faces among the attendees, which boosted my interest. Dad keeps attending these yearly conferences where the top CEOs and executives of many multinationals in India keep sharing their inputs on taking one's business to new heights. Their vast experience in

their chosen field is unmatched, and I am upbeat about learning some of the tips myself.

Though I am the CEO of one of the largest multinationals headquartered in London, I am always open to learning new ways to improve my company's efficiency. The seats are comfortable, and the room is well air-conditioned. I can see people clutching the lapels of their coats due to the cooler temperature, but I am used to it. I have been in London since childhood, and that city is my home.

The conference begins with many eminent speakers coming on the stage to share their experiences. Just as I lower my head to check on my phone messages, I hear the sultry voice of the next speaker. Raising my head, I look around the stage to spot the owner of this ethereal voice, and within seconds, everything about her captivates me. Dressed in a black tight pencil skirt and a crème casual top tucked at the waist, her hair tied into a ponytail which keeps bobbing sideways whenever she points to the projector screen to explain something, she is the epitome of beauty with brains. She has skin-coloured stockings covering her smooth milky legs and the pencil-heeled sandals adorning her feet. I am mesmerized by her elegant and sophisticated way of dressing. Instead of paying attention to the insights that she is sharing, I am busy staring at her eyebrows, the way they twitch as she explains the incoming questions and the gestures of her hands as she convincingly puts her point across. She has a soft smile on her glossy pink lips as the crowd cheers and claps for her as she ends her presentation. Thanks to the large plasma screen at the corner of the hall, I could observe and admire each movement of her goddess-like body.

I clap with the rest of the audience as she takes the front row seat next to an elderly gentleman who congratulates her on the speech.
"What is her name?" I ask the person sitting next to me since, in all this ogling, I missed hearing her name.
"Tanisha Gupta."
"Tanisha…" I smile.

And the next minute, I surf her details on my phone. She is the CEO of Gupta Industries and has taken the helm of her company from a young age after her father passed away too soon. There are numerous articles about her various accomplishments, and seeing her in her professional get-up makes me want to know everything there is to know about her. She is also a motivational speaker and has proven records of inspiring women to start their own businesses. I am awed by her commitment to her work, and what attracted me the most was her dedication to growing the company her father had started.

Just two hours back, I wasn't even aware of this woman. And now that I am, I can't wait to know everything there is to know about her.

****

<u>Few Hours Later</u>

I hit the Receive button on my Skye app to connect the video call on my laptop with my parents in London. They make it a point to call me every night.

"Hey, Dad. Hi, Mom."

I finish drying my hair with a towel before putting it away.
"Sameer, did you shower just now? Isn't it too late there?" Mom inquires.

Yep. It's almost midnight. I usually took a shower earlier, but today I was too engrossed in gathering all the details about Tanisha Gupta. I learned about her inner circle of friends and family and came to know that they call her Taani. Such a cute name!

"Yeah, I was busy, Mom. How's everything over there? Did Dad take you out for dinner tonight?"

Mom frowns at Dad as though expecting him to respond to my question.

"Sameer, my meeting got extended, son, and I couldn't take her out. But I promised we'd go out over the weekend. You know your Mom hates it when I break my promise to her."

Mom rolls her eyes while answering that.
"Your father knows everything, yet he can't stop from committing the same mistakes again."
"I am sorry, Darling."

Dad raises her hand and kisses her fingers, and Mom blushes, admonishing him. To date, she feels embarrassed when Dad kisses her openly before me. They have always been a perfect example of a romantic couple and are my inspiration. I also want to have the same kind of love and compatibility with my future partner. *With Tanisha...* Damn!! From where did that name pop up? Why did I think about her again?

"How was the conference, Sameer?" Dad's voice breaks my trance. "Was there anything new for us to implement in our business?"
"A lot, Dad. I'll talk to you about it tomorrow."
"Yes, enough of your business talks." Mom chides. "This is a family call, and Sameer, I want to ask if you checked out the profiles I emailed you. I liked them all. Pick one and make her your bride. I can't wait to see you get married."

Indian Moms will never stop pushing their children to get married soon. I too look forward to getting married soon, and that suddenly brings another thought to my head.

"Umm, Dad. Have you ever heard about Gupta Industries here in India?"
"Oh, yes. I have heard a lot of good things about that company's progress in recent years. Tanisha Gupta is the CEO of that company if I am correct."
"Yes, and she was one of the speakers at today's conference. What a woman, Dad!!" I smile, praising her oratory skills. "She's quite impressive, Dad."

Dad is intrigued as I don't usually get impressed very soon, and never at the first meeting.
"It looks like she has left a mark on you, Sameer." Dad teases.
I try not to grin and turn to look at my mother instead.

"Mom. Can you send my alliance for her? I mean, I read somewhere she is single and-"

"This is the first time you are initiating sending your marriage alliance to a woman. I am sure Tanisha is the reason behind it. She must be really good."

"Mom, you have forwarded me innumerable profiles of girls, and none of them appealed to me. But the moment I saw Taani at the conference today, all I did is think about her, and I'm desperate to have her as my life partner. Mom, you remember you always told me that sometimes all it takes is one look at a person, and you know they're the one for you? She is the one for me, Mom. I'm sure of it. I am deeply drawn towards her." I wink at my Mom and Dad. They both are surprised by my eagerness to take this alliance forward.

"Sure, we will do it right away, son. We have a common social circle through whom we can get to know about her." Dad mentions. "If she is the woman my son wants, I'll pray to God that his wish gets fulfilled because I know whoever you marry Sameer, she'll be the luckiest woman in this world. We know what kind of a man we have raised, and we are so proud of you."

It's a blessing to have parents who inspire me to be a better man. Their motivation keeps me going. We talk for some more time, and I am back in bed, dreaming about the woman I hope to know more about with every passing second.

****

Three days later, when I spoke to my parents again, they gave me some unexpected news.
"What do you mean she does not want to get married?" I ask them. "Did she reject my profile?"

"No, Sameer. We didn't speak to her directly. We talked to Narayani Kapoor. Taani has a close relationship with the Kapoors. Narayani Kapoor's grandson, Vansh Kapoor, is Taani's best friend."

My heart skips a beat.

"Just a best friend?"
"Yes, Sameer. They are just friends, and the Kapoors are the only ones she has as her family now. Her half-sister, Vidhi Gupta, came to India recently and is now staying with her. So, Taani is looking for prospective grooms for her sister. She is not willing to marry until and unless her sister has settled down."

Oh, okay. That doesn't sound like a problem but a solution, in fact.
"Then forward my alliance for Vidhi."
"What?" Mom snaps. "You like Taani, not Vidhi. Then why do you want us to do that?"
"So I get to meet her, Mom. I want to get to know Taani better. And that is only possible if I am in her inner circle of friends. Going by the traditional method of befriending her will take a long time. This is a sure-shot way of being around her."

I know I am confusing my parents. But I am very clear about this. I want to meet Taani and get to know her, and I'm willing to go to any lengths to make that happen.

CHAPTER 2

Taani

Sameer Khanna. I'd heard about him before. His family is based in London, and they are in the Advertising Business for more than two decades. His proposal had come for my sister, Vidhi, and ever since the Kapoors had approved him, I haven't been able to take my eyes off his profile. Damn! *The man is handsome.* Of course, I trusted the Kapoors, and they would never ill-advise me, yet I couldn't stop myself from digging more into his details the night before we had planned to meet him. Yes. *We!* Vidhi was not going to meet him alone. I was accompanying her so I could assess him before she made any decision. Vidhi is new to this country, and being an overprotective sister, I could not let her go to meet an unknown man alone at night. And my best friend, Vansh Kapoor, was also joining us. Obviously, I'll need company if Vidhi and Sameer get along well with each other.

My heart skips a beat at that thought. Suddenly the image of Sameer Khanna eyeing my sister fills me with rage, something that has never happened till now. I can't be jealous of my own sister. I have no plans to find a life partner and marry anytime soon. Then why the hell do I feel heartbroken at the thought of Sameer Khanna and Vidhi together and finding each other appealing? I shrug off these silly thoughts from my head for the moment. Now it is even more important for me to meet this man personally and know if he is really suitable for my sister.

****

I wore a turquoise off-shoulder dress for dinner with Sameer, Vansh and Vidhi. Vansh picks us up from my mansion. He is in a grumpy mood tonight, and I think it is due to his hectic work schedule. I notice both Vansh and Vidhi throwing daggers at each other through the rearview mirror, and I think it's because Vidhi doesn't trust or like my best friend Vansh's protective nature. They always bicker when we are together, and at times I strongly feel like they have some unresolved issues from the past, which is not possible considering I met my sister, Vidhi just a few weeks ago. After my Mom died when I was young, Dad married Vianca Holler, a woman he met in Austria. Vidhi is their daughter. My maternal aunt didn't trust my stepmother to look after me, nor did Vianca Holler made any effort to take me into her fold. Though Dad tried his best to keep us all in touch through phone calls, that connection broke when he passed away. I had no contact with either of them until years later my stepmother contacted me to entrust Vidhi's responsibility to me. Vianca Holler was suffering from the last stages of pancreatic cancer. She wanted Vidhi to marry someone from India, and I was happy to help them. Therefore,

Vidhi, having grown up in Austria, could not have met Vansh. But hold on; didn't Vansh also go to Austria a few years ago? Gosh! Am I missing something here? Or maybe it's all in my head, and I am overthinking, as usual. Vansh is my best friend, and if he had known Vidhi in the past or if anything was going on between them, he would have definitely told me. I immediately shrug off that possibility and look forward to our dinner.

We enter the plush five-star hotel Sameer is staying at and make our way toward the restaurant. I immediately notice Sameer, and our eyes meet for a fraction of a second before he comes forward smiling at Vansh. Sameer is wearing a casual navy-blue jacket with a blush pink shirt and tight-fitted jeans. I know blue is his favourite colour as I had read it on his profile before, and I am twinning with him today, though not exactly in the same shade. Unknowingly I had picked his favourite colour to wear tonight when technically it should be Vidhi doing that.

I glance at Sameer and all those Google photos just don't do justice to his handsomeness. With his hair in a stylish cut, his smart attire, his well-groomed French beard and a twinkle in his eye as he looked at me, this man was beyond perfection. I am sure Vidhi is also impressed by his first look because as soon as Vansh shakes hands with him, Vidhi gets all flustered. Why the hell am I uncomfortable with her reaction?

"Nice meeting you, Mr. Kapoor."
"Call me Vansh."
"Okay," he smiles.
"Nice meeting you, Vansh. Ugh…" Sameer turns

towards Vidhi and me as if waiting for Vansh to introduce us.

"This is Taani Gupta and her sister, Vidhi," Vansh mutters.

Sameer smiles charmingly at me, looking straight into my eyes, and I feel goosebumps erupt on my skin. What the hell! I never thought a man's smile could make my heart flutter like this. I quickly push Vidhi forward and re-introduce them.

Sameer shakes hands with her. I feel a little miffed that he did not do that with me. Shit! I quickly remind myself that Sameer is here to see Vidhi, not me. Vansh and Sameer lead us to our table, and Vansh pulls out a chair for Vidhi while Sameer does the same for me. His fingers brush my bare shoulder as I take a seat, and I jerk in surprise at the spark of fire coursing through me. Sameer stills for a moment, and I could see he is equally surprised by that spark between us, but he quickly covers it up and takes his seat. The conversation begins. Vansh and Sameer talk about the latter's business in London, and soon the topic shifts towards Vidhi and how her choices are in perfect sync with those of Sameer.

By the end of the dinner, I know I am jealous of seeing Sameer and Vidhi talking nonstop, laughing together as if they are already comfortable with each other, even though I feel it's just a friendly conversation for now. When I turn to Vansh, I see his mood is off, just like mine. I pinch his arm gently to get his attention.

"Why do you look so serious?" I whisper to Vansh. "I'm good. My mind is at work. Nothing else."

"He is good, isn't he?" I am curious to know his viewpoint on Sameer because, as far as I can see, there is a connection between Vidhi and Sameer. I hope Vansh proves me wrong.

"They've just met, Taani. Have patience. Don't form your opinion so soon."

Vansh is right. I shouldn't be linking them so soon. Vidhi will tell me later whether she really liked Sameer or not.

Sameer orders his favourite dessert and wants us to try. It's very sweet and though I do not have a sweet tooth, I still relish it. Strange! Is it because I liked the man that I have started liking his choices too? Shit! What the hell am I thinking? I am here to match Vidhi and Sameer, but my amorous feelings for him are leading my mind astray. This has to stop.

I quickly rise from my seat, nudging Vansh to follow me, as that's the only way we can give Vidhi and Sameer some time alone to talk in private. I pretend to have some work with Vansh, who seems unhappy to leave Vidhi alone with Sameer. I get he doesn't want my sister to be alone with a stranger at this hour. But I'm also sure that Vidhi will be fine. Sameer seems to be a good man. Sameer looks disappointed when he realizes that Vansh and I plan to leave them alone but soon composes himself and promises to drop Vidhi safely home once they finish their conversation. Did I really notice the disappointment on his face? Was it because I was leaving? I wish! *Stop it, Taani.* I scream at my subconscious mind to get rid of these silly thoughts.

"Taani, can I have your number? I don't have your

number in case I need to call you regarding any further development."

I am surprised Sameer wants my number and not Vidhi's. But again, it makes sense he would need the contact number of Vidhi's family if he wants to take things forward. And I am her only family.

"Sure, I will text my number. Save it."

I already had his number saved as Vansh's grandmother, Narayani Kapoor, forwarded it along with his profile last week. I quickly text him my number and see him smile as he saves it on his phone. What does this mean? Wait! I should stop analyzing all his actions and focus on my goals. The moment Vansh and I are out of sight, it is possible Sameer would start flirting with my sister. The mere thought of him and my sister angers me, but it doesn't stop my mind from thinking about him. Why am I so intrigued by this man? I've never been this desperate for a man's attention before.

I remain quiet as Vansh drives me home. He is also silent. I get down from the car and ask him if he wants to come inside and have coffee, but he refuses on the pretext of some work and drives away broodily. It's strange the way Vansh is behaving these days. I was always his go-to person when he wanted to talk about his feelings and the problems bothering him, but these days I find him lost in his world. Why? Though I want to ask him about that, I don't push him as I know he will come back to me one day on his own.

****

It's been more than an hour since I got home. I have already showered and am currently pacing in my living room, waiting for Vidhi to return. Sameer was going to drop her home, he had said. I don't know why I am still nervous. I am also eager to know what happened after I left the hotel. What did they talk about, and did she feel that spark with him? Somewhere in my heart, I regret leaving them alone. If I were there with them, I could have helped them get along better, or I could have prevented them from progressing any further. Oh, God!! What am I even thinking? How can I wish for Sameer to dislike Vidhi? I guess I'm just over-exaggerating my thoughts. I know I am being very edgy, but I can't help it. Is it because this is the first proposal that Vidhi has agreed to, or is it only because I don't want Vidhi to like Sameer and go ahead with this proposal? Shit! I can't be that selfish, can I? I really need to rein in my thoughts before I mess things up.

The sound of a door opening breaks my thoughts, and I see Vidhi entering the living room. Judging by her mood, I think she is confused and stressed, but the moment she sees me, a smile appears on her face.

"Hey, you are awake?" she asks.
"I was about to go to sleep," I lie. "Did Sameer drop you?"

Vidhi swallows nervously before replying.
"No, a friend of mine did. A little after you left, this friend of mine called me to meet, and since it was already late, we decided she would pick me up from the hotel and drop me home. That way, we got to spend time and catch up with each other."

Oh! I am confused. Which friend is she talking about? It's not even a month since she has been here in India, but I don't cross-question her and instead come straight to the point.

"So, what have you decided about Sameer?"

Vidhi shrugs.

"It's too soon to make that kind of a decision, Taani. He is an amazing guy. But I want to take this slow. Is that okay with you?"

Slow? Does that mean she likes Sameer and wants to explore this relationship before she gives her approval for the wedding?

"Sure," I smile, cupping her cheek. "Take all the time you need. I'm glad we have progressed towards the promise I gave your mother."

At the mention of her mother, Vidhi gets teary-eyed and hugs me. It is a reminder that my prime duty is to find Vidhi a partner, not snatch the one she is interested in. That's it! This little conversation with her has opened my eyes. Whatever happens, I need to stop thinking about these absurd feelings I keep getting when we talk about Sameer or even when he is around me. Henceforth, I will see him as Vidhi's suitor only and hope I will be able to keep my feelings at bay.

CHAPTER 3

Sameer

Tanisha Gupta! Ever since I met her, she's constantly been on my mind. She looked stunning, like a gorgeous mermaid in that turquoise blue dress she wore when we met. Technically, it was supposed to be my first meeting with Vidhi, and I had already made plans to grill Vidhi subtly about Taani, her likes and dislikes, to get to know her better. But when I came to know Taani herself was coming along for dinner to meet me and make sure I was worthy of her sister, I couldn't contain my excitement. I was yearning to shake hands with her, but instead, I shook hands with Vidhi after Vansh Kapoor introduced us. And dear lord, I was thrilled to notice a little disappointment on Taani's face when I didn't shake hands with her. She looked upset at being left out, or was it my imagination? Vansh Kapoor, Taani's best friend, had joined us too, and for some reason, I hated the fact that Taani was so close to him. I am fine with them being best buddies, and to be honest, I felt Vansh was totally into Vidhi, which is confusing. Did he like

Vidhi? If that's the case, why can't he straight away speak to Taani and ask for her sister's hand in marriage? I am sure Taani wouldn't mind unless she has feelings for him. Nope!! That thought leaves a bitter taste in my mouth. Taani is Vansh's best friend only. Period.

It was only yesterday that I had taken Taani's number, and I wonder if it's too early to chat with her. I don't want her to think I am desperate for her sister because that's not true at all. Vidhi is a sweet woman, but she only gives me sisterly vibes whenever I see her. My heart beats for Taani, her elder sister and the woman I am interested in. I keep pondering for some time before dropping a message to Taani as I see her online on WhatsApp.

Sameer: Hello.
She instantly replies.
Taani: Hi.
Sameer: I hope I am not disturbing you.
Taani: Not at all. I wasn't doing anything.
Sameer: That's debatable. I've heard Tanisha Gupta doesn't rest enough and is always doing something or the other.
Taani: Did Vidhi tell you that?
Sameer: Who else? And if it's true, you should slow down. Get a break.
Taani: I wish I could. You know how it is to run a business single-handed.
Sameer: Isn't Vidhi interested in joining you in the business?
Taani: She needs time. She is learning the basics and is doing really well.
Sameer: If you need any help, I am always here. I've heard people say I am quite brilliant.

Taani: Is it? Then, I'm afraid you'll have to compete with me because I'm brilliant too.

Sameer: Two brilliant minds make an excellent team.

Taani: You are funny.

Sameer: You haven't seen my funny side yet.

Taani: I think you are right. Why don't you come for dinner tomorrow? In that way, you and Vidhi can get to know each other better.

There my mood sours again. Can't Taani see I am trying to know *her* better and not Vidhi? I specifically took *her* number. I am chatting with *her* right now. Isn't it obvious I'm interested in *her* and not her sister? And she says people call her brilliant!! Either she is really clueless about the hints I am throwing her way, or she is purposely overlooking my advances. But I would be a fool to miss this golden opportunity of dining with her at the Gupta villa, and therefore, I agree.

Sameer: Done. I'll be there.

Taani: Cool. What kind of cuisine do you prefer? I'll have my chef prepare your favourite food.

Sameer: I've heard you surf a lot about the people that interest you. So, surprise me, Taani Gupta.

Taani types something and then stops. I can see the three dots on the chat conversation appearing and disappearing. Finally, after a minute, she replies.

Taani: See you at our home tomorrow evening. You'll be amazed by my surfing skills, and that's a promise.

Sameer: I will be waiting. See you tomorrow then. Now get your beauty sleep. Good night.

Taani: Good night, Sameer.

And our first chat conversation ends. I keep reading and re-reading her messages. Soon these formal, bland messages will turn into naughty and romantic ones; I will make sure of that. Gosh! I have it bad for her, and I can't wait to meet Taani again for dinner. This time, I will give her a sure hint that I want *her* to be my life partner and no one else. It is pretty evident that she is equally attracted to me. I don't mind if she wants to wait till Vidhi gets settled in life. I am ready to wait for Taani for eternity.

****
<u>Next Day</u>

It's highly frustrating and unfortunate that I have to cancel my dinner plans with Taani at Gupta villa, and that too at such a short notice. One of my clients has preponed the video conference that was to happen tomorrow morning, and him being an important client, I could not ignore it. The moment I learned about the change in plans, I immediately called up Taani to inform her, and she was pretty understanding about it.

"Sameer, it's totally fine," Taani mentions over the phone, but I can sense she is upset with the news. Was she equally excited to meet me as I was? "I know despite being the CEO of our company, at times, we don't have control over our own schedule. It's completely okay if you can't make it for dinner tonight. We will plan this some other time."

I am impressed by her maturity.

"Do you know that you are a rare species, Miss Gupta?"

"Now I am a species to you, Mr. Khanna?" she teases me back in the same tone. "Let me warn you, if things work out as planned, you are going to be married to a Gupta woman."

"I know," I say with pride. "I promise you that will happen, and I can't wait for it."

Taani is speechless for a minute, and so am I. It's hard to predict what she is thinking at this moment about my declaration, but whatever I said is the truth. Under no circumstances am I letting Taani walk away from me. The more time I spend with her, getting to know her, the harder I fall for her beauty and charm. It's about time I stop confusing Taani that I am interested in her sister.

"Umm, I'll let Vidhi know you aren't coming for dinner tonight."

Taani's voice interrupts my thoughts. She is back to her composed self. All that magic we had between us a while ago as we conversed is lost. I think her mind is at loggerheads with her heart. She is attracted to me but is willing to ignore this attraction as Vidhi is the one I had proposed to meet. I wish I could tell her the truth that the proposal was just a means to get close to her. I want to clarify that I am not interested in Vidhi but her. But this is not something I can do over a phone call. I need to have this conversation with Taani face to face.

"Yup. You guys enjoy the delicious dinner cooked specially for me. I'll be happy to know someone relished all that yummy food tonight, if not me."

"I don't think you need to worry about that. Vidhi and I are going to feast on it. You take care of your clients, and we'll speak again later."

"See you later, then," I repeat.

She goes silent again.

"Bye, Taani."

"Bye, Sameer."

She feels that invisible pull between us, doesn't she? I pray to God she does.

****

After a restless night dreaming about Taani, the morning came with a respite. Dad called with the good news that the deal we were trying to finalize for the past few months was finally ours. It's the best news I have received as this will mean tremendous profit for our company in the coming year. The moment I end his call, I think of throwing a small party as a thank you to our company executives here in Delhi, as they have played an integral part, working tirelessly on this deal. I convey this to my Dad, who encourages me to go ahead with the party without them. It would be the first time I would throw a party without my parents attending it. This party would also be an excuse to invite Taani over and spend some time with her. Ever since I have made my interest in Taani known, my Mom is behind me to know how far I've come to winning Taani's heart.

"Mom, it's not as easy as you think," I tell her again when she asks me about it on a video call while I get dressed for the event tonight.

"Sameer, until she knows you are there for her and not Vidhi, she will never take you seriously. Let her know the truth as early as possible, son."

Mom is right. That is exactly what I plan to do; use tonight's party as an excuse to open up my heart to

Taani. I wear my charcoal black suit jacket and turn back to my laptop screen.

"Alright, I will tell her tonight. Now tell me, how am I looking?"

Mom passes me a flying kiss.

"Handsome as always, my boy."

And this is why I love her the most. She is good for my ego. I give Mom a flying kiss and wind up the call. I do not want to be late for my own party.

****

The image of Taani in a wine-coloured, spaghetti strap gown with a thigh-high slit, her hair cascading down in waves over one shoulder, leaving her neck exposed to my hungry eyes, is enough to burn my body with a raging fire. Her classy style has always lured me since I met her. But so far, I have always seen her in casual or business outfits. Tonight, dressed in shimmery party wear, she is the most gorgeous woman present here. Taani is wearing a thin platinum chain which is hardly visible on her milky white skin, but the wine-coloured heart-shaped pendant matching with her gown that rests just above her neckline is an eye-catcher. She and Vidhi are both at the entrance when they see me. They make their way toward me while greeting their friends, which gives me enough time to calm myself and avert my eyes from Taani's beckoning curves beneath that dress. I'm not very particular about women's curves, but I have a fetish for the ones Taani possesses.

"Hey, beautiful ladies," I greet Taani and Vidhi as they reach me, my gaze sweeping over Taani from head to toe. I love what she's done to her eyelashes.

They look fuller and curvier tonight. "Thanks for coming."

"How could we not?" Taani smiles back and nudges Vidhi to talk to me. Didn't she get my hint that I am not interested in Vidhi?

"I am upset with you," Vidhi speaks.

"What did I do?"

"You cancelled our dinner plans for your boring client call."

I laugh heartily at her comment.

"Sorry, but I couldn't skip it. And you are right. It was boring. I would have had more fun dining with two beautiful women instead. But, I am disappointed by you too, Vidhi. In these two days, why didn't you call me even once? I thought we were friends now."

She looks disoriented as if finding an excuse. I don't know, but I have a feeling Vidhi is not really interested in any marriage proposals Taani or the Kapoor family are showing her, including mine. But then, why is she doing this?

"Sorry! Tell me, how can I make it up to you?" Vidhi asks.

I think for a few seconds before smiling back at her. Tonight, I want to tell Taani about my interest in her, but before that, I have to speak to Vidhi so that she too is aware of my liking and can help me woo her elder sister.

"Be with me throughout this party, to begin with. I really want to introduce you both to my friends." I declare.

"Hmm..."

"I said both of you, Vidhi; you and Taani. Just stay with me. I have never been lucky enough to have two beautiful women around me all at once."

Taani raises her brows. "That doesn't sound very nice, but since you have been a gentleman so far, we might just agree."

I lean towards her, and anyone looking at us could easily detect a spark between us.
"Trust me. I'll never disappoint you," I whisper in her ears.

Taani looks startled at my sudden closeness, but before she can retreat, Vidhi interrupts us.
"I am dying to meet your friends. Where are they?"

She says this glancing at Vansh Kapoor, who is also invited to this party. This definitely arouses my suspicion and curiosity. Maybe, just like I have some secrets, Vidhi too is hiding something, and I am sure it has something to do with Vansh.
I turn to Taani, waiting for her response. Her interest in meeting my friend circle is also important.

"Yup. Lead us, Sameer Khanna," Taani nods, bringing back my smile.
"This way, ladies."

I happily lead them and introduce the Gupta sisters to my friends. Taani is way too formal with them, whereas Vidhi happily mingles with everyone. I see the difference in both the sisters. Taani is an introvert, whereas Vidhi is the exact opposite. Taani gets a call and excuses us, and I am left talking to Vidhi and my friends, but I still have my eyes on her.

She looks adorable when she scratches her eyebrows while speaking on the phone as if thinking about something. She senses my gaze on her and looks in my direction, her eyes burning into mine. We stare at each other before she averts her face and continues to talk. I focus my attention back on Vidhi, who looks slightly uncomfortable with my friend, who is clearly flirting with her. I am overcome with a protective brotherly feeling and pull Vidhi towards me and slide my arm around her waist to signal my friend to back off.

Just as the conversation ends, I see Vansh Kapoor walking towards us. Taani greets him with a hug before he can reach Vidhi and me. He smiles at her and returns her hug. That friendly gesture between them leaves a sour taste in my mouth. I don't mind Taani and Vansh's friendship, but until I know her feelings for Vansh, he will always make me jealous.

"Sameer," Vansh shakes hands with me formally. "You have quite a big group here. I must say, you are exhausting my girls."

"Your girls?" I frown. Taani senses the tension between us on Vansh's remark, and she quickly intervenes.
"Vansh is very protective of Vidhi and me. After all, we are family, aren't we?"
Vansh nods.

"In that case, from now on, they are my family too." I proclaim, and my comment baffles the three of them. If I marry Taani, she will be my wife, and her sister, Vidhi, will automatically be my family. And Vansh is their best friend. He will be like a family member too. I grin at the thought of me being closer to Taani than Vansh. Call it male pride or anything else, but this feeling makes me one happy man.

"Dance with me." Vansh grabs Vidhi's hand and pulls her away from me. I did not expect that, or maybe I did. If he wanted to dance, he could have asked Taani to be his partner as they are good friends. Why her sister? This confirms that something is amiss between Vidhi and Vansh.

Taani looks amused as Vidhi willingly goes with him.

"Sure, but…" She looks at Taani, who smiles back.

"Go ahead. I'll be fine."

"Of course, you will be fine because you'll be my dance partner," I declare. It's time Taani knows my interest is in her and her only.

Taani looks at me, confusion and excitement written all over her face, and then at Vansh, who drags Vidhi towards the dance floor. They do have something going on. But, for now, I am going to enjoy this beautiful opportunity to dance with Taani Gupta.

"Are…are you sure?" Taani hesitantly asks me after Vansh and Vidhi are gone. "I mean, I am not very good at ball dancing."

"Is that an excuse to refuse my dance proposal?" I tease, and she laughs.

"No, I am serious. I try to stay away from the dance floor as much as possible."

"And why is that?" I ask, curious to know the reason and thankful that not many men have danced with her.

"That's because I always happen to stamp my

partner's foot with my pointed heels whenever I dance."

She looks embarrassed to admit that, and I can't control my laughter.

"Sameer," Taani hits my chest.

"Alright," I control my laugh. "But two things. Firstly, even if that's true, it is completely normal."

"And second?" she waits for me to complete.

This time I move closer, crossing that thin line of privacy between us.

"I don't mind if you stamp my foot, but I hope you don't stamp my heart."

Her ruby red lips part in confusion as she sees the raw desire in my eyes for her. Before she changes her mind or gets skittish by my advances, I hold her hand and lead her to the dance floor.

CHAPTER 4

Taani

Never in my dreams did I think Sameer and I would be dancing to a romantic ballad. It's weird because he should be dancing with Vidhi. But she is with Vansh, looking quite cozy, grooving to this intimate song. I shift my gaze to Sameer again and find him staring at my face while we slowly dance with each other.

"You dance well for a beginner," he flirts, and I wonder why? Sameer is not the kind of a man who would give me undue attention if he wants to marry my sister, but every time we are together, why do I feel he is more interested in me and not her? Is it my imagination? I am confused.

"Wait a few more minutes, and you'll soon change your opinion."

I turn again to glance at Vidhi, and she is still dancing with Vansh.

"Eyes on your partner, Taani," Sameer whispers, leaning closer, and my eyes widen in surprise. Did he say *'partner'*? "I mean, it is bad manners to dance with someone and not look at them," Sameer clarifies.

"I told you, that's why I always stay away from the dance floor. And by the way, I was just checking on Vidhi."

Sameer grins.

"You are babysitting her if that's what you do all the time. Vidhi is a grown-up woman and can look after herself. But I like that you are so warm and kind towards your half-sister. Not everyone is as cool and accepting as you are."

No one has ever told me that before. Sameer is the first. When he praises me for my kindness, I feel warm with a sense of pride filling my senses. Dad always used to praise my kind disposition when he was alive. Vansh and the Kapoor family also did, but there is something in the way Sameer mentioned it tonight. It is as though he is really proud to know me and be with me.

"Well, you hardly know me, to be honest. At times I am more than kind, but often I am a strict disciplined woman who is used to getting things done her way, every single time."

"Is that so?" he chuckles. "Guess what? I am like you, too. I know exactly what I want, and I don't rest until I get it, be it at any cost."

His arm slides around my waist, drawing me closer. He is not touching me inappropriately, but it is definitely not what I expected from Sameer. It could also be a simple dance move. I ignore a thousand thoughts that enter my mind.

"Do you like Vidhi?" I come straight to the point.

Since his family got this alliance for her, I need to know Sameer's thoughts regarding my sister.

He realizes I purposely diverted the topic and loosens his grip on my waist, but still holds me close. I can smell his cologne due to his closeness. It's a heady, musky scent wreaking havoc on my senses.

"She is cute, friendly and easy to talk to, unlike you."

Sameer flicks his finger on my nose.

"You are a tough nut to crack, Taani. Why is that?"

Did he just touch my nose? That's a cute gesture.

"Someone has to be tough. Besides, you are speaking as if you have never come across any tough woman before in your life."

Sameer twirls me in sync with the music, only to make me land on his chest as we continue dancing.

"If you want to know how many casual relationships I have had so far, you can ask me directly. Don't sugarcoat your words, sweetheart," he winks.

"Smart!!" I mouth, blushing at his endearment. "I am just making sure we make the right decision before progressing any further with the proposal."

I am being honest, and Sameer also has no intention to lie.

"Alright, if I say I have had three casual relationships so far, will it be too much for you to process? Will I still be eligible in your eyes?"

Three relationships? He has stayed abroad all his life and is a handsome man. Of course, he is no saint.

Women might be throwing themselves at him at every opportunity they get.

Sameer tucks a strand of hair away from my forehead.

"None of them lasted for more than two months," he adds.

Two months is a short time which makes me doubt his long-term commitment. Is he commitment-phobic? I am sure he must have had genuine reasons why those relationships didn't last long. Seeing the worry laced on his face by my silence, I decided to tease him a bit.

"Why? Why did they leave you?" I ask playfully.

Sameer frowns at first and then realizes I am making fun of him. He relaxes a bit and continues to dance.

"First one left me as she found a better catch in a famous musician and fell in love with him. The second one was a bit clingy and very high maintenance in terms of her tantrums, so obviously, I couldn't continue with her, and the third one, she was already dating someone behind my back, which I came to know later on and so I broke up with her. She was simply behind my money and name. Since then, I have been single. Dad and Mom wanted me to find someone to settle down with and have a companion I could come home to. They couldn't see me whiling away at this age, so they somehow convinced me to get married in an arranged alliance."

"And that's how they proposed for Vidhi?" I interrupt.

He looked a bit nervous, which I suppose is because he just admitted his past relationships to me.

"Forget about me. Tell me about you, Taani. Why haven't you married yet?"

"I haven't found anyone yet who could catch my eye."

"Really? I don't believe you."

"That's your problem, then, not mine."

I poke my finger on his chest and look away to find Vidhi, who has disappeared from the dance floor along with Vansh.

"You know I can read faces?"

Sameer's voice brings my attention back to him.

"Stop bragging about yourself, Mr. Khanna. I have surfed a lot about you and haven't read that anywhere."

He laughs.

"Trust me. I can. At least those faces that interest me. I don't know about the rest, but I can definitely guess why you haven't married yet."

Alright! Now I am curious. What theory has he come up with?

"Okay, why am I not married yet?" I demand to know, wanting him to try his luck at guessing.

"Not like this. If you want me to read your face, you will have to keep looking deeply into my eyes for a minute without thinking about anyone or anything else. Only then I can focus."

My heart skips a beat. Look into Sameer's eyes for a minute? If I do that even for a second more, I will not be able to stop myself from falling for him. God only knows how I have forced myself to accept the fact that he is Vidhi's suitor, not mine, and that I have to stay away from him.

"C'mon, Taani. Give me this chance. I promise you won't regret it."

His confidence in reading my face baffles me. Besides, a part of my heart is jumping in joy to know about his thoughts and feelings for me, which I understand is wrong on my part, but I can't help it. I still want to know.

"Fine," I nod. "Go ahead."

We stay quiet for a long moment, gazing into each other's eyes. Despite the loud music in the background, all I can hear is my heart beating frantically. It's never happened to me before. Looking into Sameer's eyes and seeing the fire dancing in his intense gaze is giving me goosebumps. My cheeks heat up on their own when I see how keenly Sameer is looking at me. I hope he doesn't see me blush. I have never been this close to a man before and always thought it would be awkward when the time came for me to be intimate with someone. But with Sameer, I don't feel any awkwardness. On the contrary, it feels like I am home. *Like he is my home.*

"You are a workaholic," he begins. "And you feel your dad has left a huge responsibility of the company on your shoulders. You want to desperately make him proud wherever he is by taking the company to a greater height."

Oh my god. Sameer is on point with his observation. No one has ever read me so aptly before. The next instant, Sameer cups my face while his eyes continue to look into mine. I believe this is his way of reading my face further.

"You think a relationship will divert you from your goal, so you have never tried getting into one, even if you wanted to. You are scared, Taani Gupta. You're terrified of becoming merely someone's girlfriend or wife, losing your identity and dividing your responsibilities. And not because you think you can't handle it, but because you don't want any more hassles in your life than you currently have."

My eyes brim with tears. He is right. I am scared. I might put up a show of being strong and a control freak, but underneath all that bravado is a scared Taani who doesn't want to take the risk of getting involved in a relationship that can take her focus away from running her company.

"But you are wrong," Sameer continues. "A relationship doesn't weaken you. If it's with the right man, it will only make you stronger, and you can still achieve what you want to without the fear of not being able to handle the two together. Imagine the day you make your Dad proud. Do you think your Dad would be happy seeing you all alone that day? Don't you think on that particular day, you'll also yearn for someone dearer to you to share your success with? Someone who can laugh with you and shed happy tears for you, someone who can pat your back with pride, give you a tight hug and celebrate your victory?"

The tears I have been holding in my eyes till now roll down my cheeks. I've never been so vulnerable with anyone before. Not even with Vansh, then how could I break down before Sameer? What is this unnamed feeling I have for him, and he has for me, which draws us together, making him read me so well? Whatever this is between us, it feels beautiful, it feels right. The moment Sameer's thumb wipes my tears, I want to flee from this place. I don't want him to see me in this state any longer. The mask which I wear in front of the world is also what I want Sameer to see. I can't let my weakness, my insecurities, my fear and my emotions out to anyone, not even to Vidhi, Vansh or Sameer.

I push his hands away and quickly make my way out. Fortunately, Sameer doesn't follow me. Thank God!!

****

The entire night I thought about Sameer and how he understood my feelings which I had never shared with anyone before. What was this man doing to me? He was not supposed to get close to me. He should be wooing Vidhi. I felt like I was betraying my sister even if Vidhi hadn't shown much interest in taking this alliance further. But this has to stop. My heart's dilemma is on one side and the promise I made to Vidhi's mother on the other. I can't break that promise at any cost.

I wanted to ask Vidhi again what she had decided about Sameer, and if she was thinking about him, but I didn't get time to do that as the next day I had to suddenly take a flight to Udaipur, where my German clients had landed. They would be in

Udaipur for two weeks and wanted me to visit them to discuss the further developments of the deal. Frequent and unexpected travel like this was not anything new to me. But at present, I was happy this little seclusion from my home and from Sameer was enough to give me time to sort out my feelings and the self-control which I had started to lose around him.

****

Udaipur is a beautiful city, and so is the Lake Palace Hotel, where I am staying for the next three days. It's almost 9.00 pm when I complete the check-in formalities at the hotel and turn towards the elevator to crash into my room. I am exhausted and plan to order some room service before hitting the bed. Entering the elevator, I press the button to my floor, and just when the door tries to close, someone presses the outside button, halting the elevator again. My body stills on seeing the man entering inside with a carefree attitude and a smug smile lighting up his entire face as he gives me a quick once over. In grey athletic shorts and a sleeveless white vest covering his upper, sweaty body, giving me an ample view of his ruggedly bulged biceps and his strong muscular legs, is Sameer Khanna. He looks like he is coming straight from the gym, and good lord, he looks deliciously edible. *Stop it!!* I shut my rambling mind before snapping my gaze at him as the elevator doors close.

"Sameer?"
"Hi." He smiles briefly at me before sipping some water from his gym bottle.
"What are you doing here? Are you… are you stalking me?"

He doesn't bother to reply and continues sipping the water from the sipper. The way he drinks the water from the sipper, making gurgling sounds of satisfaction, makes me warm to my core. What the hell is he up to?

"I can ask you the same thing, Taani," Sameer interrupts my naughty thoughts. "Are you stalking me? What are you doing here in Udaipur?"

Really? Does he want to play the blame game now? I cross my arms.
"I came here to meet my clients."
"And I came here to meet my friend, who needed my advice and my company."

Which friend is this? I am curious. I wish I could ask him that. Is he here with a woman on a holiday or something? Is that why he didn't mention his trip to Udaipur yesterday at the party to me or anyone else?

The doors to the elevator open, and we both get out on the same floor.
"What's your room number?" he casually asks.
"103. And yours?"
"106."

The moment we reach our floor, I realize our rooms are opposite each other. I don't think Sameer is a playboy who would bring a woman here to have a clandestine weekend or something, but the curiosity is killing me. I try to fake an issue with my room key while he opens his room door easily.
"Umm. I think there's something wrong with my room key. Would you mind if I … come to your room and … I mean.. make a call to the reception?"

Sameer stares at me, bewildered for a second. Not giving him time to think or process his thoughts, I push him away and enter his room to inspect it. The room is neat and clean, just the way I like to keep mine, and there are no signs of a woman or any girly belongings, which means he is alone. I turn to find Sameer glaring at me. *Oops.* I think I made my suspicion quite obvious this time.

He reaches me, and before I can find some excuse, Sameer snatches my room key and walks out. He swipes it at my door, and it opens easily. Sameer turns around towards me and hands me the room key.

"Sameer... I was..."

The cool breeze of the air conditioning is not enough to cool my burning body as Sameer grabs my arms and pins me to the wall next to the door.

"The friend I am here for is *you*, Taani Gupta," he mutters. "I didn't come here with any other woman for a holiday. I came here for you because you have serious misconceptions about yourself, and I know none of your friends has even been able to spot them. I might be a stranger to you, but sometimes the way we open up to people we hardly know is much easier than opening up with the ones closest and dearest to us."

I am in a daze, staring unblinkingly at him as he says all this. I have never had any man care for me and my feelings to this extent, let alone stalk me to another city. I stare at Sameer blankly as he continues.

"Last night, I didn't follow you after our conversation, despite seeing you in tears because I knew you needed some time for yourself. But that doesn't mean I am letting that matter go. I take you and your sister as my family now, and whether you like it or not, I want to be there for you both even if you don't ask me for any help."

"You think I need help?" I murmur, trying hard to sound normal.

"I think you need a break from all the business and family pressures you have surrounded yourself with right now."

I roll my eyes looking towards the door, but Sameer pulls my chin up, forcing me to look at him again.

"I am not talking about a normal break, Taani. A break where you discover who you really are and think hard about what you are missing in your life. You need time away to do some soul searching. I am here to fix that even if you don't want me to. I am not going away this time, Taani. Even if you throw me out of this hotel right now, I will keep coming back."

He seems very determined to find the real Taani Gupta amidst this controlled businesswoman I have become.

"My life is perfect, Sameer. This is exactly how I want my life to be, working mindlessly, and putting all my passion and efforts into my work. I know where this is coming from. Had I been a man doing the same work, you wouldn't think I am missing something. That's the way our society is, always discriminating against a woman. It is okay for a man to work hard and provide for his family, whereas when a woman does the same thing, they wonder if she is leading a normal life or not?"

"You think I give a f*ck to what the society thinks?" he yells. "I was raised by a working mother, who at one point in time earned more than my father. It was only later that my dad's vision and dedication turned him into a successful businessman. Only after that did Mom take a break to nurse me and make sure someone was home to look after my needs as Dad was away working hard."
Oh! I didn't know that about his parents. I thought he was born rich.

"Taani, whatever you are doing professionally is something we rarely see women doing. It's great, and we all are proud of you. But I want you to focus on your personal self also. I have heard you don't even take breaks and are always working like your life depends on it."
"That's my ambition, Sameer. And I don't see anything wrong with it."
"Losing yourself in the process is wrong."

I understand his point. I have literally not taken any break for myself in the last few years. All I did was work and more work to bring the company to the position where it is now.

"You have already made your Dad proud. Now make him happy by giving me your next three days."

Next three days? What does he mean? Sameer reads that query on my face.
"I know you are here to meet the clients. I won't stop you from working. But after work hours, you are

going to be yourself. You'll be Taani Gupta, the girl you were until your father was alive, and not the CEO Tanisha Gupta that you are now."

My mouth hangs open at his demand. Can I really do that?? Or rather, can Sameer Khanna bring out the old Taani in me again? Can I handle both my versions together from here on? And most importantly, why is Sameer so interested in bringing me out of my self-imposed shell?

CHAPTER 5

Sameer

Taani looks at me with a shocked expression, like I have proposed to her. Well, that will happen too, but it has to take a backseat for now. Blurting out I am not interested in marrying Vidhi, but her, is not going to be easy until I convince Taani to take a break from all the responsibilities, she has surrounded herself with and to prove to her that she too deserves a chance at love. If I told her the truth now that it's *she* I desire, the first thing she is likely to do is to prohibit me from contacting her or her family, which I can't risk at the moment. I know she is not looking for marriage now, and I totally respect and understand that. But until she starts thinking about her life minus her business, in terms of her personal life—which I know is non-existent—and brings to the fore her real self, she will think about me. That is why I am here. To help show Taani what she is missing out in her life and how beautiful life could be with a loving partner by her side.

"Are you this intrusive with everyone you know?" she asks, bringing my attention back to her again.

I have caged her to the wall in between my strong arms and she hasn't resisted yet, but by the look on her face, this isn't going to be as easy as I thought it would be. Convincing Taani Gupta of anything is no less than moving a mountain. But I am Sameer Khanna, and I can even move Mt. Everest for her if it's going to bring a positive change in Taani's life.

"Only for special people, and you are my top priority right now."

I'm sure she will argue that Vidhi should be on my mind, and thinking about her should be my top priority. So, before she opens her mouth, I shut her up with my words again.

"C'mon, Taani. Three days. Am I asking too much? Just give yourself three days to be what you could have been if the responsibility of handling the business wasn't on your shoulder. Forget who you are, forget who I am to you, or on what basis we met. Right here, right now in Udaipur, I am just a friend who wants to get to know the real you. I want to be the one you can open up to and act and speak about whatever has been inside you for years. Sometimes, it is more therapeutic to talk to strangers than to your own people. Give yourself these three days from your life, Taani Gupta."

Her resolve is almost breaking; it's written on her face. Her ruby red lips part on their own, and I can't help but fix my gaze on them, imagining what it would feel like to touch those lips with mine, to devour them to my heart's content.

"Give me your three days, Taani."

My fingers itch to brush her cheeks, and after seconds of controlling them, so as to not embarrass her with my actions, I finally give up and cup Taani's face in between my palms. She is taken aback by my gesture, but I needed to do this to convince her.

"Please, Taani. You deserve it, and I'm sure your father would want you to be happy."

She shuts her eyes, her stiff body slowly melting by my gentle touch on her face and she leans her cheek against the warmth of my palm. I know she wants to give herself a chance to live freely again the way she did before being burdened to live up to her father's expectations. And if I am right, the thought of freeing herself never crossed her mind until tonight. But it's Taani Gupta we are talking about, and I have heard she is the toughest nut to crack. The tenderness in her expression diminishes as she opens her eyes and stares into mine for another second before pushing me gently away from her.

"Good night, Sameer."

And she leaves my room as if totally unfazed by the moment we just shared. I stare at her receding back with my heart leaping out of my chest, my jaw clenching at the unsuccessful attempt. But this is not going to deter me. I will not rest until I make sure Taani balances her life, keeping herself above and over anything and everything.

Taani

I don't understand Sameer at all. He is not even remotely speaking or thinking about Vidhi. From the moment we met, his behaviour screams to me that he is more interested in me than her. Initially, I thought it was just in my head, and I was overthinking, but by following me to Udaipur, he had proved my point. I couldn't sleep the whole night, which is obvious as Sameer's words and his determination in making me spend these three days in Udaipur doing things that I could have done if I did not have this huge responsibility on my head, kept haunting me. A part of my heart knew he was right. Had Dad not left so suddenly, I would have enjoyed my life a bit more. I didn't even complete my graduation when he died, and the company was already crumbling in losses. It was the board of directors and Vansh's uncle, who helped the company sustain itself until I was capable enough to take over the reins in my hand. Obviously, no one believed I could do it. I was hardly 23 when I officially took over as the CEO, and had no prior experience. People mocked me, and employees started quitting thinking I wouldn't be able handle the huge responsibility, and just to prove them wrong, I got so engrossed in my work that I forgot I even had a personal life. Dating was out of the question, as was admiring a man beyond a party. All of it felt like a burden considering I knew I had so many other duties to attend to, and I couldn't indulge in getting into relationships. I wasn't that girl anymore who would chat late nights with her boyfriend, hang out with him at pubs, go for dinners and meet and greet his family and friends. A relationship needed time and effort, and though I was ready to put my heart into it, my mind would always be somewhere else. This is exactly why I kept pushing my marriage plans ahead, even though Vansh's grandmother kept on asking if she could find a groom for me.

The doorbell rings the next afternoon just as I am back from my meeting with the German client.

"Ma'am, these came for you."
The hotel attendant gave me a small yellow tulip bouquet along with a card attached to it.
"Thank you."
Shutting the door, I check the card which I believe would be from my client or the hotel management as a courtesy of my stay here, but the moment I read the words, I know who they are from.

Five Tulips for the woman who is going to let loose and fulfil five of her desires in the next two-and-half days. All the best. I hope you give me the opportunity to be a part of this journey with you, and to meet the real Taani Gupta, the woman you have caged in your heart for this long.

Your well-wisher,
Sameer Khanna

I stare at the bouquet with five yellow tulips. How did Sameer know I loved tulips? I am sure I have never mentioned that in any of my interviews or social media posts. Even Vansh and Rohan, my best friends, didn't know about it. Whatever it is, Sameer is not going to back off. If he wants to be a part of this journey in making sure I live my life as before, so be it. I adore how he is hell-bent on knowing the real version of me without any filters, exploring myself and being the woman, I always yearned to be. I stare back at the tulips and quickly text Sameer that I am ready to introduce him to the real me and ask him to meet me sharp at 08:00 pm in the lobby. We are going out.

When I messaged him, little did I know he would come to my door at 08:00 pm to escort me personally? Sameer smiles at me. With his dark black eyes and his sexy French beard, wearing blue jeans and a crisp white linen shirt neatly tucked in, Sameer is undoubtedly the most handsome man I have ever seen.

"I can't believe I am agreeing to this," I tell him to break my chain of thoughts and to stop myself from touching his two-day-old stubble.

"This is the first time you are doing something for yourself. Be happy. Are you coming out in this?"

Sameer gives me a once-over.

"What do you mean?" I look down at my maroon skirt and the white shirt, but it seems my attire has not met his approval. "Isn't this dress good enough?"

Sameer exhales audibly and leans at the doorframe.

"It is perfect for the CEO Tanisha but not for Taani, who will fulfil her first wish of being her old self."

I know what he means.

"I packed only formals for this trip."

"Then let us go and buy what you haven't packed. C'mon."

He grabs my hand and leads me out. The moment our fingers interlace with each other, I already get this feeling he is mine. Sameer Khanna is making a place in my heart faster than I had imagined. Before I could think about its consequences, he presses the elevator button and smiles at me.

"What is your first wish, by the way?"

I ignore my thoughts and grin because I know what his reaction will be after I tell him.

"Gol Gappe competition."
"What?"

I laugh at his shocked expression as he leads us inside the elevator once the doors open.
"Are you serious?"
"I am. You have no idea how much I enjoyed doing this with Dad when he was alive. It is a thrilling experience to compete with someone to have maximum Gol Gappas, and mind you, Mr. Khanna, I always win."
Sameer is still stunned by my revelation.
"Alright, if that's what you love doing, we will start with it. But who are you going to compete with?"
"You."
His jaw hangs open in shock.

"Cat caught your tongue, Sameer? Should I return back to my room and drop this idea of-"

"We are doing this," he declares before leading me out of the elevator towards the lobby. I glance at him in awe. One thing I have learned about Sameer is that he is a man of his word. I wonder how he will complete the challenge with me, though.

We first drove to the nearest mall where Sameer shopped for dresses of all kinds; traditional, western, casual etc. This man is on a shopping spree today.

"We are taking this one too," he says, picking two more dresses for me. "And this one here is cute. I like the colour."

He keeps picking a few more dresses when I grab his arm.

"Sameer, what are you doing? People are staring at us."

He gives a quick glance around and shrugs.
"So what? They are not the ones paying for it. If given the time and liberty, Miss Gupta, I would buy this entire store for you."
The words slip out of his mouth while he continues his shopping, oblivious to what he just said. He would buy this entire store for me? And why is he investing in picking up dresses for me is another question to ponder. I have never seen a man shopping with so much delight for any woman.

I stop him from embarrassing us further and drag him away from the Women's section.

"Wear this tonight," he declares, giving me a pair of black jeans and a noodle strap sky-blue crop top.
"This? I'll look like some teenager if I wear it."
"That is what I want you to feel throughout your journey of fulfilling the five wishes, Taani. Now go. You are wasting time."

He pushes me into the trial room and I don't even have the time nor the energy to argue with him. He is right. To be the Taani I used to be earlier, I have to feel like one first, and these casual jeans and top are perfect.

We buy ten dresses, all different styles, before driving to where you get the best street food in Udaipur. Sameer looks at me as I anxiously stroll to pick the most hygienic stall to eat. I have never been this excited to eat in local eateries as I am today. And that too my favourite street food, Gol Gappe. As a businesswoman, I have always kept a strict check on my diet and exercise regime. I've almost stopped eating street-side food, but tonight is the time to let loose. I can already feel the adrenaline rush in my body. Getting into the groove of the old Taani is feeding my soul with renewed vigour. We pick a stall and order two Gol Gappe plates to start with. As soon as I eat the first one, I moan in pleasure, closing my eyes and relishing the sweet and spicy taste as I swallow the whole thing down. When I open my eyes, Sameer is staring intently at me with fire dancing in his eyes. The air of attraction swirls around us, and I feel that pull between us again. Unknowingly, we were drawn to each other ever since we first met. Sameer wipes off the extra liquid of the Gol Gappa that oozes from the corner of my lips, and my body freezes. He keeps doing that until my face is clean again, and his hands linger for a moment longer on my lips before he takes them away. To break the moment, I turn to the stall vendor and ask him to keep filling our bowls with the Gol Gappe until we ask him to stop.

"How did you know I love tulips, and that too yellow ones?"

"You do?" he sounds ecstatic.

"C'mon, Sameer, it can't be just a guess. Did someone tell you I loved yellow tulips?"

"No."

He eats his fifth Gol Gappa, whereas I am on my 7th already.

"My Mom loves yellow tulips, and whenever I see you, I remember my mom. She's a kind, generous, confident, possessive woman and, at times, full of tantrums, just as you are. So, I thought your liking would match hers, and thank God it did."

I hit his arm gently.
"I throw tantrums?"
"That's what you are doing now. Stop thinking about everything else and focus on the competition. I am not letting you win this time."
"Try me."

I start gobbling faster than him while Sameer laughs on seeing my desperation to win. In fifteen Gol Gappes, Sameer clutches his stomach, his eyes and nose red from the heat of the spice, and declares defeat. I was already on my 18th Gol Gappa, and that means I won. I jump in joy, feeling at the top of the world after winning this competition again after so many years. And in all my excitement, I lean forward and give him a tight hug.

"I'm so loving this thrill," I say, snuggling closer to his body, and I suddenly realize what I have done. Sameer and I are not even proper friends, and he is the suitor of my younger sister. I shouldn't be doing this. I pulled away from his body, even though I wanted to be held close, and it took an enormous amount of courage to look back in his eyes. Sameer hadn't completely engulfed me in the hug, and I wonder why? He knows his limits, and so should I. We stare at each other for a long time, thinking of a million things we shouldn't be doing. What is it about him that makes me want to throw caution to the wind and enter into a relationship with him for real? His phone rings breaking our stupor. Sameer takes out his phone and answers it almost immediately.

"Hey, Mom."

Mom? Now that I know what a gentleman Sameer is, I can't wait to meet the parents who raised him to be one.

"I am out with Taani." He mentions smirking at me.

He told his Mom that I am with him? Won't they think why we are out at these odd hours? His mother requests a video call, and though I am flustered, Sameer connects the call. He speaks to her, and I ensure not to intrude and stay away from the phone camera, so I am nowhere visible in that video call.

"Sameer, you are eating at a local joint? You know street food upsets your stomach," his mother scolds, and as soon as she does my jaw drops.

Sameer rolls his eyes.

"Mom, one night of eating on the streets is not going to affect me. And please, my stomach is absolutely fine since I came to India. The food here is lovely."

"You mean to say I don't cook well?"

He laughs at her remark.

"No one can beat you in cooking, Mom. C'mon, you know that. Now let me introduce you to Taani. Hold on."

Sameer tells me to come near and speak to his mother. I am a bit confused, nervous, and, most importantly, annoyed at him for not telling me he has a delicate stomach and has issues eating local street food. I glower at him and stand next to him with a smile on my face.

"Hello, Aunty," I say, smiling at Sameer's Mom. She is in her mid-50, as Vansh's grandmother had told me, but she still looks so young and fit.

"Taani," she sounds pleased. "It is so nice to see you, sweetheart. How are you doing? And how's your meeting going on in Udaipur?"

Does his mother know why I am here? Who told her? Sameer?

"It's going great, Aunty, but I want to apologize to you first. I didn't know Sameer shouldn't be eating on local streets. We just had Gol Gappas, and he didn't say anything when I dared him to compete with me. I am so sorry."

His mother chuckles and then turns to Sameer.

"Sameer, I am sure you lost the competition, but take some medicine tonight before you hit the bed, and Taani, you don't need to apologize. Sameer is a strong boy. Being a mother, I can't help being worried about his diet as this is the first time he is so far away from home for a long time."

A mother's worry never ceases. I can understand that but have never experienced it as I lost my Mom too early in life. Tears gush in my eyes, and I try to control them.

"Sweetheart, why do you look so sad? Did I say anything wrong?"

Sameer turns to me, and as if it's habitual, his palm strokes my arm and then my back.
"You spoiled her mood, Mom."
"She didn't," I wiped my tears and glared at him

for saying that to his mother. "Seeing your worry reminded me of what I am missing in my life. My mother."

Sameer's Mom sighs in disappointment.

"I'll sort that problem for you. Henceforth, whenever you feel like speaking to your mother, call me. I am always available for you, sweetheart."

"No way." Sameer rejects the idea. "I am not sharing your number with Taani, or else you will reveal all my past blunders to her."

That cracks me up, and I laugh. We all laugh. So easily, Sameer and his mother cheered me up. I am sure this family is perfect for my sister if we go ahead with the marriage. Suddenly that leaves a bitter feeling in my heart. I'll lose Sameer, and this feeling that I can associate only with him, when he marries Vidhi. But that's the reality. Whatever I am doing right now is temporary. Sameer belongs to Vidhi, and that's never going to change.

****

The next day, during breakfast, Sameer asks me about my second wish on the list that I could never fulfill before.

"Walking on a ramp dressed to the nines, wearing the sexiest outfit with all the focus lights on me."
He literally drops his spoon on the plate, and I roll my eyes. Is that too much to wish for?

"You wanted to be a model?" He inquires, and my smile tells it all.
"I wanted to do modelling at some point in my life, but then you know how my priorities changed. And I

don't regret not being one. Modelling is a very demanding profession, and I don't think I could do enough justice to it. But that's not the point, Sameer. For once, I would like to live that feeling of walking on the ramp. I don't mind not having an audience because I really cannot attract attention and let them see how the CEO of Gupta Industries is flaunting herself without any cause or a reason. I know it all sounds crazy. We are in Udaipur, where we do not have any sort of arrangement."

I look down and continue eating the cornflakes. When I look back at Sameer, he is already typing something on his phone, a grin appearing on his face. "You don't worry your pretty head about it. That will be arranged." He assures.
"Really?"
"Yup, but I hope you have something sexier packed in your bags, or we might need to go shopping again."

Who is this man? How did he arrange a ramp walk for me? I check my watch.
"Umm, not much time for shopping. I have a meeting in an hour, and I won't be free until evening."
"Then, I'll shop for you." He suggests so casually as if he has been doing that for me for ages.
"Are you sure?"
"Sure as hell! Plus, I can always call Mom and take her help in selecting the sexiest outfit for you tonight. Let me know when you are back, and the dress will be ready in your room."

I swallow nervously.
"Sameer, nothing fancy, okay? I mean, this whole idea of ramp walk is already weird, and you shopping for the outfit-"

He immediately grabs my hand over the table and squeezes it with assurance.

"I'll never get anything that makes you uncomfortable, Taani. Trust me."

My mind was already in a foggy mess, and the way we held hands and his assurance was enough for me to lose control over myself. I squeeze his hand back like he did mine and smile at him. It's a smile full of gratitude for being relentless in giving me this little happiness I never knew I would enjoy so much. Sameer Khanna is stealing more than just my heart, and I am afraid to admit that if this continues, I might be at a point of no return.

CHAPTER 6

Sameer

I didn't have to repeat myself because I knew I was falling hard for Taani. The simmering attraction I felt for her initially had metamorphosed into a raging inferno. I gave her a piece of my heart every time I looked at her. I'm glad she didn't walk away from the idea of reliving her old self, something she couldn't do so far, and I am delighted Taani allowed me to be a part of that journey with her. I could see the happiness on her face yesterday when she won the Gol Gappe competition. I would brave my stomach ten times over and let her win, if I could bring this level of immense joy to her life. The shock and regret on her face when she came to know about my plight after eating street food made me happy that she was equally worried about my health as my mother was. Since that phone call last night with Mom, Taani was constantly messaging me if I was doing well and if she could get any medicine to help my upset stomach. To be honest, I am fine, even more so, as today we would be fulfilling Taani's second wish on her bucket list, *to walk the ramp.*

Mom helped me select the best outfit for her, and I knew how gorgeous my Taani would look wearing it. Her beauty doesn't need any definition; it is incandescent. It glows brightly like a shining star whenever she's around. I haven't met a woman who is bold and beautiful, sweet and sexy, free yet controlled, tough yet vulnerable, all at the same time. Taani is what I have always been secretly yearning for my whole life.

I had arranged the ramp walk for Taani at the same resort we are staying at. They had a beautiful garden facing the lake where a make-shift ramp was set up by the event management company I hired. They had done a brilliant job in creating the ambience of a fashion show. Taani was escorted from her room to a small dressing area behind the stage, where she would change into her outfit and get her hair and make-up done, giving a feel of the green rooms at fashion events. The dress I bought for her was a striking charcoal black colour gown in soft silk, with a fitted bodice and a thigh-high slit at the side. The evening gown had a plunging neckline, and I hope Taani wasn't uncomfortable or nervous wearing it. I was excited to see her in a dress of my choice. I had arranged for the stylists and the make-up artists to give Taani a complete makeover. I wanted her to enjoy this evening and remember it for a lifetime. I could imagine her surprise and awe at the quick arrangements I had made specifically for her. I had booked the entire garden area, giving us complete privacy so there wouldn't be anyone else seeing her walk the ramp in that outfit except me. I wanted her to feel like a star today, so I had specifically instructed the ramp to be well lit with focus lights to catwalk, giving her the feeling of being a showstopper.

I wonder if Taani wasn't burdened with the company's responsibility at such a young age, would she have made modelling her career? But one thing I am sure of; whatever she chose to do, success would have kissed her feet.

"Why are there no lights here?" I shout at the event coordinator, who quickly turns on the stage and ramp lights, and I see Taani posing at the far corner, waiting for my approval to walk. She looked breathtaking in that shimmering black gown clinging to her body like a glove, showing off her perfect curves. Her hair was parted on the side, leaving it open, big hoops dangling from her ears, and a small chain with a single solitaire adorning her swan-like neck, the diamond resting between her ample cleavage, and my body immediately hardened. I had to remind myself to breathe again. I give her a subtle nod to begin her walk, and Taani gets the affirmation she needs. The background music turns on, signalling her to walk the ramp in a way she always dreamt of. She falters and hesitates at the first step. She looked shy, nervous and utterly mortified to put on this exclusive show for me, whereas I couldn't stop myself from staring at the vision in front of me. Taani walking the ramp in this stunning gown, looking directly at me, is igniting a fire in my body. As she glides towards me, she gathers her wits and catwalks like a star, with an air of confidence I have never seen on her before. Taani slays the ramp leaving me hot and bothered because no matter what, I know the only thing I am allowed to do is to ogle her. I can only undress her with my eyes, even if I am dying to touch her soul through her radiant and supple body. What's wrong with my libido these days? My body is in a constant state of arousal whenever I am around Taani. I'm literally aching for her by the time she reaches the end of the ramp. She gives me a flying kiss as she would to an audience and jiggles her hips to the music, flaunting herself as she sees the plasma TV recording the entire walk and displaying it on the screen before her. She then turns around and sashays back to where she had started.

I want to follow and drag her to the next wall available and crush her lips with mine until she is breathless, devouring her entire body with kisses and slamming into her, thrusting hard to relieve myself of the ache in my lower body. But this is not about me. We still have a long way to go before that happens of her free will. For now, I raise my hands and clap for her, showing her how much I loved her performance.

I immediately rein in my thoughts as she gets down the ramp and comes running towards me, where I stood mesmerized by her beauty. Before I could think of anything else, Taani jumps at me with joy and hugs me tight.

"That was an out of the world feeling, Sameer. Thank you so very much."

I remember her hugging me after the Gol Gappe competition last night, and I won't repeat my previous mistake. This time, I hug her back, holding her quivering body in my arms, breathing in her sexy scent. I love seeing her deliriously happy because of me. Her smile makes my heart sing, and I feel so protective of her. I promise to always look out for her, no matter what.

"I don't know how to say this and how many times," she whispers with a smile. "But thank you so much. All my other wishes I could have fulfilled any day in the future, even on my own, without your help. But this—to model and walk the ramp—I couldn't have done it alone, even with my wealth and fame. It would have never occurred to me to have my own personal ramp and to put up this kind of a show. It was possible only because of you, and I'm so grateful for making my long-forgotten dream come true. You really outdid yourself in creating this magic for me, which till now was only a dream."

"Dreams do come true, Taani Gupta. All you have to do is open the door when they knock," I whisper.

She pulls herself away and a grin.
"Knock." Taani nods in excitement. "That's exactly what my third wish is. To knock myself out, boozing without the fear of getting sloshed. I trust you, and I know you'll drop me safely to my hotel room if I can't make it there by myself. Won't you?"

Of course, I will. But I am shocked.

"You amaze me, Taani Gupta. I couldn't have imagined out of all your desires, drinking till you pass out would be one of them."

She feels embarrassed for a moment but continues her explanation.
"Every party I attend and pick up a drink, I have to remind myself to be sober and drink in limit. I am the

CEO of Gupta Industries, and people look up to me as their inspiration. I don't want to tarnish that image. Not to mention, I always have a tight work schedule in the morning, which means I can't afford to wake up late with a hangover. I have been a controlled drinker all my life, but not tonight."

She pinches my cheeks.

"You have given me wings, Sameer Khanna, and I want to fly. Tell me you'll be there to catch me if I fall?"

"Do you even need to ask?" I answer, my palm stroking her cheek. She's so soft and sensitive that I can feel her shudder at my touch. I know she wants to shut her eyes and enjoy the feeling of me touching her, but she stubbornly forces herself to keep them open while I continue. "I will never let you fall, Taani, and even if you do, I'll always be there to catch you, every single time."

Taani's gaze lingers on my face a bit longer than necessary before she pulls away from me.
"I'll change, and until then, you decide where we are drinking tonight."

Before I can even comprehend, she rushes to the changing room.

****

"This is for my Papa." Taani raises her fifth shot of Vodka in the air to make a toast.

We picked the in-house bar of the resort for completing Taani's third wish. She knew exactly what drink she wanted to start with, and soon she wanted to try everything she hadn't tasted so far. I am off alcohol tonight, sipping on lemonade to ensure I drop her safely to the room. Taani is on a roll, and I must admit, a drunk Taani is a treat to watch.

"Cheers to Papa," she makes me raise my glass, and we clink our glasses together.
"Cheers," I repeat.

Taani gulps the entire liquid in one shot before laughing heartily. She is blabbering nonstop, and is not in her senses. For the past half hour, she has repeatedly told me she loved her dad very much. I know she does, and that's the reason she wants to take his legacy forward by bringing her company to the fore.

"You know Sameer, when I used to be sad, Papa would cocoon me in his embrace. Like really tight..."

She enacts by hugging herself tightly.
"Like this... Very tight..."
I nod, understanding her feelings behind it.

"And then he used to stroke my hair telling me things will be fine again because nothing is permanent in life," she adds.

I swallow nervously, seeing a tear roll down her cheeks.

"Not even life," she murmurs, picking the next shot and gulping it down her throat.

I try to wipe her tears, but she shoves my arm.

"And then he left me," she sobs. "He left me to be on my own, Sameer. I miss him so much."

I feel for her. Taani might be surrounded by her sister, best friends and extended family, but she is missing that warmth in her life and is probably still searching for it.

She puts her glass away and gets down clumsily from the high chair. Then, coming near me, she stands between my legs.

"You are the only one who saw me. You saw that I was missing something in life."
I keep staring at her as she continues, stroking my cheeks with her knuckles. Taani is tired and sleepy, and I know she is about to doze off any moment now. "How can you read me so well, Sameer?"

I grab her wrist and pull her closer to me without breaking our eye contact.
"We have a soul-to-soul connection, Taani, and it's not just from this birth but the previous one. I can feel it. Can you?"

The moment I utter those words, she cuddles my body. I put my glass away and hug her back with the same passion. I keep stroking her head with love as she cries her heart out.

"It's okay," I hush to ease her cries. "We all face worse things in life, Taani. But always remember, they only make us stronger and wiser. That's what your father's absence made you. You are stronger than any other woman I have met so far, and I am so proud of you."

Taani literally squeezes the air out of me as I speak, and soon her sobs subside, and her hands hang down as she falls in my arms.

I pat her cheek.

"Taani?"

She snores softly instead of responding, confirming my suspicion that she has passed out. Quickly settling the bill, I lean down and carry Taani in my arms, taking her straight to her room. She is feathery-light and easy to carry, or maybe I am too strong that I don't feel her weight. Thankfully, the staff helps me unlock her room. I place Taani on the bed while she keeps murmuring my name and continues to thank me even in her unconscious state. I take off her heels, giving her toes a gentle rub to relax her. How does she manage to wear those heels every day? Don't they make her feet ache? Ensuring she is covered adequately and the AC is at the optimum temperature, I turn off the table lamps. Taani's murmurs have stopped, and she is sleeping peacefully. I need to leave. If I wait here, even for one more minute, I might spoon her and spend the night on the same bed, which is not something she would appreciate in the morning.

****

The harsh sound of the doorbell jolts me off my bed. I was dreaming about Taani and me, how last night and every night henceforth could have ended between us, had we been upfront about our liking for one another. But this damn doorbell ruined it all. Rubbing my eyes, I make my way to the door and open it, only to find Taani standing in a pink salwar suit smiling at me.

"Are you here, for real? Or am I hallucinating?" I mindlessly ask, and she frowns.
"You are talking as if you were dreaming about me. And it's 09:00 in the morning, Sameer, and you are still sleeping?"

She is here for real, and before I could explain why I overslept, Taani continues.
"Did I bother you too much last night?"
I think for a moment, recalling all those cute moments where she made me toast like a hundred times for her father. I remembered every single second I spent with her last night—the way Taani hugged me, cried on my shoulder and found solace in my arms, and the moment when I carried her to bed—I remembered it all.

"I would have," she pouts, bringing me out of my trance. "But I don't remember a thing, Sameer. At least not after I sang the song Dad and I used to sing when I was in school."

Yes, that was the highlight of last night. Taani sang a song, and though it was off-key with slurred words, I could relate to her emotions behind it. She missed her father a lot.

"Can I come inside?"

I suddenly realize the poor woman is still standing at the door, and I haven't even let her inside. I shift aside to give her space to enter.

"You don't need my permission for that. Besides, is this your fourth wish? To wake up a sexy man from his sexy dream?"

She laughs heartily, entering my well-organized room. I like it that way, and ever since I had known about Taani's obsession with cleanliness, I made sure I was more efficient these days. I often wonder how our kids would be?

"Sameer?" Taani shakes my arm, bringing my attention back to her. "You still didn't tell me if I troubled you too much last night?"
"Even if you did, I didn't mind. Listening to you sing, toast and share your best moments spent with your father was like discovering a bit more about you, and I loved it."

She smiles a bit, hesitating.
"Vidhi has more stories to tell, and I am sure you'll love them too."
I don't reply to that and make my way to the kitchenette.
"Coffee?"
"Yes, please. How did you know I wanted one?"
"Because I was the one who kept a count on your drinks last night. You had too many to get the mother of all hangovers, Taani. How did you even wake up this early and still so fresh?"
"My routine has always been like that. I wake up on my first alarm, irrespective of how late I sleep at night."

She watches me intently as I make some coffee for both of us.

"In that case, I should keep your phone away from you every night so that you wake up when you want to, not because you have to."
"Every night?" she grins coyly. "As if that's possible."
"Try me. Nothing is impossible for Sameer Khanna, Taani. All you have to do is give me a chance."
I hand her the coffee, and though she takes a second to ponder over my words, she quickly changes her expression and sips the coffee with a casual smile.

"Vidhi is lucky to have you."

I want to throw up the coffee I just sipped at that thought.
"We are yet to decide on that, Taani and to be honest, I …"

Before I could tell her about my feelings, her phone rang.
"It's an important work call. I'll attend to this while you take a shower and dress up. I am on a spree to fulfill my fourth desire."
"Now?" I glance at the clock. It's hardly 09:15.
"Yes, Sameer. Now. Go."

She pushes me into the bathroom and quickly turns away to answer her call.

****

An hour later, we were on our way towards the Karni Mata temple, for which we had to take a ropeway. The views of Pichola Lake and the surrounding hills of Udaipur from this temple were gorgeous, and I started capturing this beauty through my camera. I clicked a picture of Taani as we got out of the cable car at the endpoint, and she immediately snatched the camera from my hand to check the pictures I had clicked so far. Thankfully, I had taken a few scenic shots, apart from capturing her candid ones.

"You still didn't tell me why you came to Udaipur, Sameer. I mean, it can't be only for me."
"Why? Why can't I come here only for you?"
"Because that's absurd. We hardly know each other."
"Then I came here to get to know you better," I wink at her, snatching my camera back and taking more pics of the scenic landscapes of the Aravalli mountains on the other side of the lake. When I turn around, Taani is staring at me suspiciously.

"Okay, if you are so interested to know, then listen. Udaipur is where my parents had come for their honeymoon, and I have heard many stories about this place and the magical time they spent here, apart from being cooped up in the bedroom. Since then, this place has held a special place in my heart. I always wanted to come here once, and when I came to know you were flying here for work, I couldn't resist joining you and giving you company."

Taani finally relaxes when she finds out I had another reason too apart from her, and though what I said was true, this visit, at present, is only for her. I wish I could tell her that. But I know, the moment I confess my feelings, she will back off from me. We have just started bonding, getting closer to each other, and I don't want her to draw the lines between us again.

"Now, will *you* tell me what we are doing so early in the morning at this temple?" I try to divert her mind from questioning me further.
"Shh, come here."

She drags me to the backside of the temple, where people are taking off their shoes to get inside.

"Don't tell me you wish to steal other people's shoes and run away?" I tease, and her million-watt smile is back.
"Shut up, and let me focus."

She keeps looking at the people coming there, taking off their shoes and putting them on the shoe rack, before heading inside the temple. I still don't understand what she wants to do, but I wait for her to enlighten me on that.
After almost fifteen minutes of keenly observing the people, Taani's face lights up. I look in the direction she is busy staring and see a woman of almost Taani's age and height, hesitating to take off her worn-out sandals before the crowd. Finally, she removes them and keeps them safely in the shoe rack before heading inside the temple.

As soon as she leaves, Taani drags me to the shoe rack and removes a pair of expensive sandals from the bag she was carrying from the hotel and replaces it with the other woman's worn-out sandals. She then puts a note along with it which I once again didn't realize she was even carrying with her.

"What are you doing?" I ask loudly.
"Shh, calm down. I am fulfilling my fourth desire."
She carefully leaves a pair of expensive sandals with a note for that woman and takes away her old ones before dragging me from that place. We both hide behind the tree trunk for some more time.
"Taani, I still don't get it," I mutter. "What did you get by replacing the new sandals with hers?"

"That." She points out to the woman who is back and is totally surprised to see the new sandals that Taani left for her. The woman reads the note, looks around and mouths a thank you, looking at the sky.

She is so happy to get a replacement for the sandals.

"What did you write in that note?" I ask Taani, who spells it out for me.
"I wrote that I wanted her to have the sandals, and it's a gift from her well-wisher friend. If she wants to thank me for it, she can look at the sky and thank me. And whenever she is capable in future, she can offer similar help to other people who truly need it."

I gape blankly at Taani.

"I have done a lot of charity, Sameer, but never on a personal level. Whatever my company does for NGOs, orphanages and other institutions is commendable, but doing something like this on the ground level is what I have desired to do for a long time. Do you know who this woman is, with whom I replaced the sandals? She works in the same hotel we are staying at, as housekeeping staff. I have seen her crossing the boutique of our resort and staring at those same pair of sandals every day. So, I purchased it for her yesterday. I had overheard her saying to her friend that she had a date with her fiancé in the coming weekend and wanted to look her best. Her salary was not credited yet, and though she had already bought a pink dress, she still had to buy a pair of matching sandals. If her salary doesn't come on time, she will have to wear her same worn-out sandals. That's why I wanted her to have the new ones, so she feels confident when she meets her fiancé. If I had given her those sandals personally, she wouldn't have taken them. Hence, I had to make sure she gets her favourite sandals without finding out who got them for her."

I was speechless. I didn't know what to say. The way Taani narrated this entire incident and the solution she found for it makes me want to kiss her right at this spot. Apart from being kind and generous, Taani has a unique way of helping people, and I still had so much to learn about her. No wonder, whatever she did, always touched my heart.

"And now comes my last wish, Mr. Sameer Khanna."

Taani breaks my chain of thoughts again.

"Which is?" I ask, clearing my throat. I am still overwhelmed by her actions and saddened by the thought that tonight is the last night we have in Udaipur. Tomorrow we are flying back to Delhi.

"You'll come to know that when we meet for dinner tonight. Until then, let's go and enjoy the city. I am going to have Rajasthani Thali for lunch. What about you?"

"Whatever you feed me, Ma'am."

She laughs at my reply, and before I know it, our fingers entwine again as we continue heading towards the temple to worship the Karni Mata idol inside.
"Oh God," I scream as soon as I see a few mice running around us. "What on earth are they doing here?"

Taani looks down and casually looks back at me.
"You didn't know this temple is also called a rat temple?
You'll find thousands of them around here in the vicinity, and it is considered auspicious if they scamper on your toes."

I jump as another rat tries to reach us.
"No way. I … I appreciate what you said, but I don't want them anywhere near me." I jump and grab Taani's hand again as soon as I see a few more near the wall.
"Why?"
"Because I don't like them."

Taani gives me a surprised look before laughing heartily.

"Sameer, the Macho Man is scared of rats, WOW!! That's news to me."

"Oh, yeah?" I snap at her, gripping her tighter. "It's not funny, Taani. People are afraid of something or the other. I am not very comfortable with rats around me. I don't mind facing a tiger or even a ghost, but rats? No way!! Get me out of this place, please."

"Alright. I got it." She holds her laughter. "I am going to post that on my social media."

"Do whatever you want to." I jump again, feeling extremely scared and restless. "Just take me out of here."
"Yup, Sameer. Relax. Hold my hand."

She leads me towards the exit and makes sure none of the rats try to cross our way again. Thank you, Karni Mata!! Taani couldn't stop herself from laughing at my expense all the way back to our hotel, and I didn't mind as her tinkling laughter filled my heart with immense joy and more love for her.

CHAPTER 7

Taani

I was in a daze since I saw Sameer diving into the pool in his navy-blue trunks. I was restless and couldn't get the image of his gorgeous body out of my mind. This man had a connection with anything blue, it seems. He really loved that colour, and I think this colour suited Sameer Khanna, who resembled a Greek God swimming in that deep blue water. After the delicious Rajasthani lunch, we reached our hotel and retired to our respective rooms. Sameer was all I had in my mind. The last three days were the best days of my life, and everything he had done for me had changed my perception of him entirely. He was kind, caring and dependable and was the perfect husband material. He had gone out of his way to make me feel alive and enjoy my life in a way I could only have hoped. Even when I was working, all I was thinking about was him, and that's the only reason I haven't talked to Vidhi properly since I came to Udaipur. I felt guilty for eyeing the man she might be interested in as her future life partner.

Sameer takes another plunge in the pool, the sound

of the splash breaking my trance, and all my insides clench on seeing his muscular body take long laps in the water. I can watch him like this with my undivided attention all my life. Who is this man? How can I be so attracted to him? I ogle his bare chest, his six-pack abs and his muscular thighs and heat pools between my legs. I feel hot all over, and I swear this warmth will make me do the unthinkable with Sameer Khanna. I stare like an idiot when Sameer sees me from the pool and waves at me. I am rooted to the spot, and despite wanting to wave back, I can hardly move my hands and legs. I realize now that I have a huge crush on this man, and this fluttery feeling pulls me toward him, near the edge of the pool. I get so lost in gawking at him that I miss noticing I've reached the edge, and with the next step, I lose my balance and fall into the pool with a huge splash. The splashing sound alerts Sameer, and thank god there is no one around here to notice my blunder.

"Taani?" Sameer rushes to me in quick laps and quickly takes me in his embrace. I feel so mortified that I fell in the pool like that. Did he realize the reason behind it?

"Say something, Taani? Are you okay? Are you scared of water?" Sameer asks anxiously, holding me close to his semi-naked torso and heat spreads in my body. I can literally breathe him; he is that close.
"I am fine… I am fine." I stutter and keep clutching his biceps to make sure we are both above the water surface. Sameer reads my confusion and leans down, and the next instant, he is carrying me in his arms and moving towards the pool steps. *Oh my God.* He

didn't need to do this. I can swim, yet, I keep gripping his body as if I can't bear to be away from him.

As soon as we get out of the pool, Sameer wraps a towel around my wet body.

"Are you okay? You are shivering."
Am I? Maybe, but it has nothing to do with the cold water and everything to do with the heat between us.
"I'll... I'll go change and see you at dinner."
"Shall I escort you to your room?"
"No." I step away. If he comes anywhere near my room, I don't know how I will stop myself from embarrassing us both. So, no thanks. "I'll go by myself. Thanks."

Before he can argue, I rush towards the door to get in the elevator. What the hell is happening to me?

****

Both Sameer and I are silent at dinner. I don't know about him, but I was lost and confused after the way my body reacted to his touch when he carried me out of the pool. I never thought I could have this scorching chemistry with someone, and now I knew, I didn't want to be with anyone else except Sameer. But he belonged to Vidhi! I shut my eyes, and the spoon falls from my hands, creating enough noise and bringing Sameer's attention to me.

"Why are you so lost, Taani Gupta?"

I keep staring at him for another minute. This isn't good. I need to detach myself from Sameer's thoughts, his touch and most importantly, get away from him until I discuss with Vidhi what she has in mind about taking this proposal. If she is serious about Sameer, I will have to effing forget him and his thoughts.

"Taani?" Sameer nudges my hand.
"Yea. Sorry, I was just thinking about my fifth desire."

I fake a smile as the idea forms right in my head. If I have to ignore thinking about Sameer, I need a distraction badly.
"Oh, yes, that's pending. Tell me." He happily asks. "What is your fifth desire?"
"Find me a partner to hang out with tonight."
Sameer looks displeased by my wish.
"What?"
"Yes," I shrug. "You know I never found time to hang out with a man before. I always kept myself busy with work and other stuff. Sameer, tomorrow we are going back home, and no matter how much I enjoyed being the 'real me', in the reality of Delhi, I have no time for that. Work pressure, my business and the rest of the responsibilities will again take priority. So, tonight I want to live freely one last time. Hangout with a handsome man, talk to him, go for a walk or a drive and have my first kiss-"

"I can't help you with this," Sameer interrupts me. He wraps his fists tightly around his fork and is looking everywhere but me. Is he jealous? He is definitely behaving like one.
"What?" I ask again. "Did I hear you right?"
"You heard it, Taani," he snaps, meeting my gaze. "I am not helping you find another man to hang out with."
"But why, Sameer? So far, you have-"

"Another man, Taani?" he interrupts me, and this time his words hit my heart. "You want *me* to find another man for *you*? Seriously?"

I am baffled. Why does it sound so wrong? And why did he stress the words 'me' and 'you'? Is he offended I am not considering him?

"Sameer," I gasp, speechless. "I... I can't hang out with you like that."
"No?" he mocks. "Then can you tell me, what were we doing together for the past three days?"
"What do you mean?" I ask, a bit shocked at his remark.
"You know exactly what I mean. Don't pretend to be clueless."
Gosh! Why is he talking in riddles? Or wait. Did he notice my growing fondness and attraction for him? Even if he did, hanging out with him is not possible.

"I really don't know what you are talking about? And it's fine if you don't want to fulfill my last desire here. Let's just ignore it, okay? And let's order dessert."

I pick the menu, trying hard to divert the topic, but before I can gauge his actions, Sameer rises on his feet, throwing his napkin on the table. He reaches me, grabs my wrist and drags me towards the exit.

"Sameer?"

When I struggle to get off his hold, he pins me to the pillar towards the washroom area.

"I have to confess something," Sameer barks at me.
"Lower your tone first," I command, looking away

from him because until he speaks nicely to me, I am not paying any attention to him.

"Look at me, Taani," Sameer chides.

"I don't want to."

He grabs my jaw and forces me to meet his eyes.

"Don't act like a coward."

"I am being perfectly normal, Sameer. You aren't. Why did you even come to Udaipur? Why did you give me these wings to be the woman I should have been when you could have spent this time getting to know my sister, Vidhi? Why did you follow *me* here?"

"Because…Because I want you, dammit." He yells, and I go blank.

He wants me?

"Are you out of your mind?" I rebuke, taking a few seconds to process what he just confessed. "Your parents brought your marriage proposal for Vidhi, and you are telling me you want me?"

Sameer grabs my hands, a bit pissed off at my constant reminder of his alliance with Vidhi.

"I don't care a damn about marrying Vidhi. It's *you* I want. It's *you* I crave. It's *you* with whom I see my future with."

I am flabbergasted by his confession.

"Yes, I want you, Taani. Just you, and I know you want me, too. Stop being so naive. We both have had this attraction towards each other since the first day we met. Don't tell me now that you never noticed."

I don't know how to process this information, so I do what I feel is the best in this situation.

"No," I snap. "I am not even remotely attracted to you, Sameer Khanna."

I push him away before he can corner me again and rush into the ladies' washroom. I need to breathe and think about whatever is happening right now with a sane mind.

Sameer

Taani is lying on my face that she is not attracted to me when I know that ever since we met, she's always had a soft corner for me, and I will prove it to her tonight. So, without hesitation, I barge inside the washroom Taani has just entered. The moment she sees me, her eyes widen. Before she can utter a word, I grip her soft hair, and bringing her face closer to mine I kiss her lush, ruby red lips. It was just a touch of lips, but heat pooled in my body. For a second, Taani freezes, but then she pulls me close to kiss me back, but this time I pull away.

"See this? This attraction between us is mutual, Taani Gupta. Stop lying to yourself about your own damn feelings," I say aloud.

The next second, Taani pulls me by my suit jacket and kisses me hard. It's like she wants to own her feelings and her attraction toward me. *Only me.* My touch on her body intensifies as I slide my palms hungrily to feel her up. I've always had a carnal desire for her curves, and today I'm able to touch them. I graze the corners of her soft breasts and keep sliding my hand down until I hold her firmly against me by her hips. Just one kiss, and she's driving me insane. I can only imagine what would happen when we carry this attraction further. The mere image of it makes me lose control, and I push her further against the grey marble wall of the washroom, grinding her with my hardened arousal. My entire body buzzes with an urgent need as Taani glides her palms over my French beard. I think she loves it, especially the ticklish feeling as our cheeks brush when we kiss. Taani's skin is hot as lava, and the low moan that escapes her mouth as I suck on her lower lip can bring me to a climax right at this moment.

I know we are in the hotel's washroom, where anyone can walk in on us, but I don't care. The woman I have desired for so long is finally in my arms, kissing me back with the same passion I have for her. How can I ever let this moment slip away? This feels like forever, and I'm ready to give up everything for this forever to last until my last breath.

A sweep of my tongue along hers, and Taani rubbed herself against my thigh as if wanting more. Her fingers tangled into my hair as I kissed her like I was addicted to those plump and juicy lips. I wasn't sure at first, but now I can tell we both needed this release badly. All those days of sneaking glances at each other, touching each other as if we were just friends and hiding the sizzling spark we always felt around each other had finally led us to this one moment where we feasted on each other's lips.

Suddenly, a bitter realization dawns and Taani stops kissing me and pushes me away. I can read the guilt on her face, and I hate that she's still thinking we did something wrong. Yes, the moment was wrong, and the way we did it was wrong, but what we did was perfect, and it would have eventually happened in due course of time.

"Taani, I..." I try to speak, coming forward, but she stops me right there.

"Don't even think of touching me again. This ... this shouldn't have happened, Sameer." She covers her mouth, feeling aghast.

"I know," I exhale in a rush, brushing my fingers through my hair. "This shouldn't have happened this way, but-"

Taani doesn't wait to hear me out and storms out of the washroom, banging the door loudly behind her.

CHAPTER 8

Taani

I return to my suite on wobbly legs, my heart racing faster than a Ferrari from the kissing marathon Sameer and I just indulged in. I touch my lips, and the taste of Sameer still lingers on. My mind and body are at loggerheads, and I want to be alone with my thoughts. Just as I enter my suite, Sameer follows behind me.

"Sameer, leave me alone," I scream.

I feel hot with shame as I realize what I have done. I feel guilty about cheating on my sister, who is probably dreaming of Sameer as her life partner. He could have been, if only I had not interfered in their lives, if only I had not got carried away in befriending Sameer and giving him the right to bring back my old self, even if it was for a little while.

"I am not leaving until you listen to me."
He shuts the door, and I am glad he did. I don't want

anyone to hear us arguing. We both are public figures, and it might attract undue attention. Why the hell did I not think about this when I roamed freely with Sameer in the streets of Udaipur for the past three days?

"I don't want to listen to anything you have to say. We did enough, you said enough, and now I am done. Just leave."
"No, I am not leaving, Taani. Not until you hear the entire truth."
"Well then, say it to the wall. I'm not interested."

I turn around to leave, but Sameer's voice halts me again.

"I was never interested in Vidhi, and that's the truth. I see her as my little sister, nothing else."

Sister? What the hell!! I turn around, annoyed and look at him.

"Then why the hell did you even send a marriage proposal for Vidhi?" I scream back.

"To get to know *you*, Taani. To woo you."

What? I am speechless. He takes a few steps ahead as he continues.
"I saw you first at the conference two months ago, and believe me, you are the only one ruling my heart since then. But when I told my parents about you, they informed me you were currently looking for prospective grooms for your sister and not yourself."

I quickly connect the dots, and my anger returns.

"You mean that proposal you sent for Vidhi was a sham? It was a ploy to get into my inner circle to find out more about me?"
"Yes." He admits shamelessly.
I reach him halfway and clutch his jacket angrily.
"Damn, Sameer, you were playing with our feelings? Why did you give hope to Vidhi when you regarded her as your little sister?"
"I didn't give her any hopes. You can ask her yourself. That night when you and Vansh left us at the restaurant, Vidhi and I only talked about you. I kept asking her about your life, your likes and dislikes, and she was happy to tell me all about you. She didn't mind it at all."

I am shocked. Why didn't Vidhi tell me all this? Sameer grabs my wrists to make sure I don't pull away again.

"Vidhi and I are just friends, and I am damn sure she isn't thinking about my marriage proposal either." Sameer exhales roughly, making up his mind to confess something else. "I think Vidhi and Vansh have something going on between them. They can't seem to take their eyes off each other when they are together."

I gape at him in horror.

"Maybe they are already into a relationship and-"

That's it. I shove his hands off me and step away.

"How dare you, Sameer? You don't want to marry Vidhi, so you are linking her with someone else. How cheap is that?"

"Taani, I am not saying this to make you angry."
"Oh, shut up," I shout back, not letting him give me any more excuses. "I won't hear a word against my sister and my best friend. They are my family, and I won't tolerate you mudslinging them. Just get out of my room."

Sameer glares at me.
"You are highly mistaken, Taani."
"Yes, I am," I nod. "I was highly mistaken when I thought you were different, Sameer. But no. By meeting me under false pretences and using my sister as bait, you have also lost the chance to be my friend. Just leave."

I turn around to conceal my uncontrollable tears. Sameer's confessions are too much for me to take in. I don't want him to see my tears, nor do I want him to believe he still has a chance to woo me. Sameer has fooled not only Vidhi and me but also the Kapoor family. I can never forgive him for that. Yes, I know I would have refused if he had contacted me directly and showed an interest in me, but if he truly liked me, he should have approached me without the deceit. I may have accepted his proposal. But now, the way he has tricked us, he has lost me forever! I hear the sound of the door closing behind me, which means he has left.

After crying for hours, I suddenly want to go home. I decided to leave the hotel at once. I called my assistant, Pooja and asked her to book me on the next available flight to Delhi. Once my flight is confirmed, I check out, leaving behind the memories of Sameer and everything we did together in the last three days. If only it is that easy to forget.

****

Vidhi is overjoyed to see me back home the next morning and I see her beaming with happiness that I hadn't seen before. I am unsure how to broach the subject of Sameer or ask her what she has thought about his proposal. If she accepts it, I'll never be able to face myself. But either way, I have to tell her that Sameer is not the right person for her. But what if she asks me the reason for declining his proposal?

For two days, these thoughts haunt me. I want to tell Vidhi the truth every time I see her, but I can't. She is also working extra hours at the office these days, and it is good to see her enjoying her role as an assistant manager in my company. Though I wanted her to be my business partner and work along with me, she chose to gain ground-level experience first before she could accept the challenging role of being a partner. I don't want to burden her either with the responsibilities I have been taking up so far. I want Vidhi to have the freedom to live her life fully. She has been through a lot of pain with her mother's sickness, and now she deserves all the happiness in life.

But I can't forget what Sameer said about something cooking between Vidhi and Vansh. I might have disagreed with him then, but when I returned home and thought about it, I recalled the times when I also felt Vidhi and Vansh's hot and cold behaviour towards each other odd. But they would tell me if they had anything going between them, right? Vidhi would still hesitate to confide in me as we have recently started bonding after she came to India, but Vansh and I have been best friends since childhood. Why would he hide it from me?

I ignore these thoughts as I pack Vidhi's bags. She is flying to Udaipur to meet the same German client I did earlier. We needed someone proficient in German to give the presentation, so Vidhi was the obvious choice. She was supposed to fly tomorrow, but the meeting got preponed. I had called her up to inform her about the change in plan. She was going to spend the night with her colleague in the latter's apartment, but now after getting to know the new schedule, Vidhi will be directly reaching the airport while I bring her bags there and see her off.

I reach the airport earlier than expected and keep looking around to see if Vidhi is anywhere, and that's when I spot her. She gets down from the car with Vansh. What is Vansh doing here? As soon as I am about to call her, I see Vansh pulling her into his arms and kissing her forehead as a loving partner would do. They are deep into their conversation when I see Vansh grinding their lower bodies together while Vidhi is laughing in delight. I couldn't believe my eyes and gasped in surprise. Sameer was right; Vansh and Vidhi are dating behind my back. But then why did Vidhi play this groom hunting game if she and Vansh are together? And Vansh? He could have straight away told me he liked my sister and wanted to get married to her. Whatever the case, this news was definitely a bolt out of the blue but since Sameer had already warned me, I was calm about it. But still, I felt betrayed by my sister and best friend.

I walk away and stand at the corner so that Vidhi doesn't realize I have seen them, and when she meets me in a few minutes, I pretend as if nothing happened and see her off with the same love and warmth I have always felt for her. But I am furious with Vansh. I will meet him tomorrow morning and find out what is going on between them. I reach my car and am about to drive home when my phone vibrates again. It's Sameer's call. He has been calling me daily since I left Udaipur and has left dozens of messages like *'Please pick my call'*, *'Don't do this to us'*, *'Talk to me,'* etc., but I ignored them. Now that I have seen Vidhi and Vansh together, I feel remorseful that I didn't believe Sameer when he told me about them. And a selfish part of my heart has again started hoping that since Vidhi is with Vansh, and is not interested in Sameer, Sameer and I can still have a future... *Together!*

Yet, the businesswoman in me, who is very adamant about not wanting a partner for now, who has no time to indulge in a love affair or marriage, prevents me from answering Sameer's calls and replying to his messages. And as usual, I disconnected the call before starting my car to get back home.

****

The next morning, I enter VK Mansion to meet Vansh, and my heart skips a beat as I see Sameer talking to Vansh's grandmother. Sameer is dressed in black jeans and a white shirt with rolled-up sleeves, showing off his tanned arms. He looks effortlessly handsome as he talks to Daadi, and I wonder what he is doing here conversing with Vansh's grandmother.

"What are you doing here?" I ask, storming inside the house.
I see Daadi and Sameer both turn at my voice, but Sameer doesn't respond to me.

"Taani, how nice to see you here. We were just talking about you."

Daadi gets up to give me a hug and while I return her hug, my eyes are trained on Sameer who doesn't shy away from me either.

"Sameer told me about your Udaipur trip," Daadi mentions, dragging me to sit next to her on the couch.
"You told her that?" I snap at him, and as he is about to respond, I shut him up again. "Just because I was ignoring you till now, you came straight to Daadi and told her everything that happened between us in Udaipur, Sameer? What kind of a man are you?"
"One minute," Daadi interrupts me. "Why were you ignoring Sameer? And what happened between you two in Udaipur?"

Hold on! Why is Daadi asking me if Sameer had already told her everything? Or did he or not? I am confused. When I look at Sameer, he exhales with a sarcastic smile.

"Always too impulsive in accusing me, aren't you?" he mocks. "I didn't tell Daadi anything about us except we met in Udaipur and roamed around the city together."
My mouth hangs open as he clarifies.
"You still didn't answer my question, Taani. What else happened between you two in Udaipur? Why do I sense something brewing between you both?" Daadi queries, and Sameer leans back on his couch, waiting for me to explain since I was the one to bring it out in the open. I really shouldn't have done that. I take a few seconds to compose myself and turn

towards Daadi.

"I am not talking about us, Daadi. I think something is brewing between Vansh and Vidhi, and I'm here to speak to Vansh," I declare.

Daadi is not as shocked as I was at seeing those two cozy together at the airport. Did she know about them already?

"Now you believe me, huh?" Sameer smirks.

I am embarrassed that I didn't believe him when he raised the same suspicion before.
"Vansh has gone out of the city this morning for some urgent business meeting," Daadi informs me. "Or at least that's what he said. Isn't Vidhi too out of the city?"
I swallow nervously.
"I am pretty sure they are together," Daadi adds, surprising both me and Sameer.
Soon the secrets start coming out. Around five years ago, Daadi had seen Vidhi's photo in Vansh's closet. That time I also hadn't met my half-sister. This confirmed one thing; Vansh and Vidhi had known each other for a long time and were hiding something from us. We tried to make sense of this information and decided to talk to Vansh's close friend, Rohan Oberoi.

Daadi calls up Rohan and asks him to come immediately to VK Mansion. At first, he did not reveal anything. But finally, after grilling him for an hour, he blurts out that Vansh had married Vidhi secretly for the Kapoor's heirloom ring five years back, and that same night, Vidhi ran away from his life due to some misunderstanding between the two. They were shocked to see each other again after five years. Vansh had no idea Vidhi was my half-sister. Now I understand why they always had this hot and cold chemistry when we were together. We warn Rohan not to tell Vansh and Vidhi that we all know their secrets about their hidden marriage now.

It hurt that Vansh had kept this secret hidden from all of us for long. That's when Daadi and I decided to finally take the reins into our hands and teach them a lesson. We wanted them to confess about whatever past they shared and what they want to do about their relationship in the future. Rohan also told us that they cleared their misunderstandings and were in love now. We were all so happy for them. Rohan took our leave as he had to take care of some urgent work, but he promised to support us whenever we needed him.

As soon as he leaves, Daadi turns in disappointment to Sameer.

"Sameer, I am so sorry that you and your family were dragged into all this unnecessarily. When Vidhi was already married to my grandson, she shouldn't have played with your family's sentiments regarding the proposal."
"She is not the only one who faked it, Daadi," Sameer interrupts. "I also never had any intentions to marry Vidhi or even think about her."
"What? Then why did your parents send a proposal for Vidhi?"
My heart skips a beat when I come to know what he is about to do. He is going to confess everything to Daadi. Sameer holds Daadi's hand in his and looks

confidently into her eyes.

"I want to marry Taani. I liked her and wanted to marry her, but since she wasn't interested in marriage anytime soon and was groom hunting for her sister, I used that to get close to her. I am sorry for hurting you all, Daadi. I didn't want to, and I am ready to accept whatever punishment you both want to give me for that."

Daadi stares at both of us. I am stunned that he so openly confessed his feelings for me to Daadi, who is silent at the moment.

"I believe Taani is already aware of all this, and hence is ignoring you since you both returned from Udaipur?" she inquires.

We both glance at each other before Sameer nods in agreement. We are all quiet again, and Sameer speaks up, looking straight into my eyes.

"I understand you are not ready to marry right now. Your other work commitments will always be your priority over everyone and everything else. I respect it all, Taani. All I want to tell you is that I will wait. Until your heart doesn't yearn for me the way mine longs for you, I shall wait, Taani. Even if I need to wait for an eternity."

I don't know why but his words touch my heart, and my eyes brim with tears. Sameer gets up from the couch without looking at me.
"I have to leave now, Daadi. If you need any help regarding Vansh and Vidhi's relationship, I'll be
happy to do so. Just let me know."

Daadi smiles at Sameer, whereas I stare at him, touched by his kindness. Despite being rejected by me and getting heartbroken, he still wants to help me sort out my sister's marriage issues? Is he for real? Am I making a mistake in not letting him in my life? I sure am!

****

I tell Daadi everything that happened between Sameer and me in Udaipur and how he managed to bring out the woman I used to be once when Dad was alive, with no responsibility on my shoulder. I tell Daadi everything except the intimacy we shared, as that is something I cannot tell her.

"Oh, dear," Daadi cups my cheeks. "When will you understand Taani that you can't live your life like this, all alone and without a partner. I know you have too many work responsibilities, but that shouldn't affect your personal life. You can't stop being happy only because you want to make your dad proud by taking his company to great heights of success."

"I don't think I can handle it, Daadi. I don't know if I can prioritize anyone over my business. And what about Sameer? His life is in London. His parents, business, friends, everything is there, whereas mine is here in India. It's too much of a risk, and while we can manage it, for the time being, I'm worried things will not go as planned for us. Dad was my only family, and after his death, I don't think I will ever be ready for another heartbreak wherein I get attached to Sameer, and then he abandons me because I couldn't make him my priority. I'm worried it'll break me beyond repair."
Daadi shakes her head in disagreement.

"Sameer is a keeper, Taani. If he could do all this just to give you happiness in Udaipur, I am sure he can move heaven on earth for you. Don't lose true love when it comes your way. It might have come by chance in your life, but if you don't take that chance now, you might never get such an opportunity again."

My heart swells with an unknown emotion. *Love by Chance!* Yes, that's what it is between Sameer and me. Will I ever be able to keep it forever? I do feel the emotional need to have a shoulder to cry on, someone who can hug me, kiss me, cuddle me throughout the night and satiate my other bodily desires too. But all these years, I was adamantly not getting into relationships. After reaching my thirties, I knew someday I would get married in the future and have kids. Then why can't I take that decision now? I might never find another man like Sameer Khanna, who is so deeply rooted in my heart in a short time. They say when destiny plans for us, it is for our best, and we should grab whatever joy comes our way. Maybe this is why I met Sameer under these unusual circumstances, and it's a sign that I shouldn't let him get away.
"It's an old saying, Taani. Marry someone who loves you more than you love them. You'll never be disappointed," Daadi adds. "Think about Sameer." She pats my cheeks lovingly, and I hug her tight, feeling disoriented at the moment.

I never hoped I would marry for love. I knew love can bloom even after marriage. But since I already have feelings for Sameer, some of which I still haven't been able to name, I think I can take this plunge with him and commit myself to someone who loves me enough for the both of us.

CHAPTER 9

Sameer

I tap my feet nervously while waiting on the plush red couch in the reception area outside Taani's cabin. I am at Infinity Tower, the headquarters of Gupta Industries. Today morning when I woke up, I saw Taani's message on my phone asking me to meet her at the office at 11:00 am. And as desperate as I was, I reached here half an hour early. She knows I am out, but since she is busy in a meeting, I don't want to intrude as I know how much her work means to her. I am losing my mind thinking about why she has called me to meet her? What does she want to talk about? Did she need help in fixing Vansh and Vidhi's marriage? Or will she tell me to back off and stop thinking about pursuing her? I hope I am wrong in my assumptions. I am secretly hoping instead of pushing me away, Taani would tell me she wants to give us a chance and see what the future holds for us. Even if she refuses to give us a chance, I will keep chasing her until she agrees, and once that happens, our family will ensure her life is filled with happiness and love in abundance.

"Mr. Khanna," Pooja, her assistant's voice, breaks

my trance. "Ma'am is waiting for you inside."
"Thanks."
I get up. If Taani had delayed calling me inside, I would have gone crazy in anticipation. I knock on her door and enter inside. She is typing something on her laptop, but the moment she sees me, Taani smiles.

"Hi, thanks for coming. Please, sit."

I remain standing. "Is everything okay with you? It looks like you didn't sleep well last night."

Taani's eyebrow twitches in surprise.

"Do you always have to read my face?"
I don't respond to that.

"What is keeping you awake at night?" I ask, sitting at the edge of her table. She looks at the way I am sitting and frowns.
"I hope this is an informal meeting," I mutter, justifying my sitting position.
"Of course, it is."

Her phone rings and she excuses herself to answer it.
"No, Pooja. Push the meeting after fifteen minutes and I'll be there by then."

Disconnecting the call, she turns to me again.
"Tea? Coffee?"
"You know my preferences already, but no thanks. I don't think fifteen minutes are enough for us to enjoy our coffee together. Some other time perhaps."
Taani nods in agreement and is about to say something when her mobile buzzes. She looks at me

as though asking for my permission to check her message, and I nod, telling her to go ahead. She sighs after reading it and looks at me.

"A reminder to attend a party at one of my client's offices tonight."

She didn't have to tell me what the message was about, but I liked that she did.

"You still didn't tell me what kept you busy the whole night?" I repeat my earlier question. This time, even though her phone buzzes, she ignores it.

"Your thoughts, Sameer. They haunted me throughout the night."

She looks at me with longing, her eyes roving over my face. I literally have to grip the table hard to prevent my hands from touching her or pulling her to me. In a high ponytail, wearing a chic black formal skirt and lavender shirt, Taani looks breathtaking.

"I see," I murmur, clearing my throat. "So, you called me here to complain about that?"

She gets up from her black leather chair and comes near me.

"This is my life, Sameer," she spreads her hand, pointing toward the laptop, her working desk, and her phone. "Back-to-back calls, meetings, conferences and events to attend take up most of my time. I don't even have fifteen minutes to myself when I am working. When I return home after handling all this, I am dead tired, and the moment I hit the bed, I am fast asleep."

"I see," I shrug. "But why are you telling me all this?"

"To let you know that prioritizing someone amidst all this will always be difficult for me. I can't be a normal wife, Sameer. Even if I marry, I am worried whether I'll ever be able to fulfill my wifely duties towards my husband and his family."

We both keep staring at each other. So, this is what Taani was thinking last night and called me here to explain it. Taani's worry is genuine, and if this is what is stopping her from taking a leap of faith in getting into a relationship, I'll ease her worry.

"Say something," Taani's voice breaks my stupor, and her impatience makes me grin instead. I circle my arm around her waist and pull her closer to my body. She freezes for a second but soon melts as my fingers brush her soft cheeks.

"I don't expect you to be a normal wife either, Taani. The way you are now is enough for me to have a future with you and only you. I know your business will always be your priority. Being the CEO of my company, I know what it takes to ensure the smooth running of the business. Fortunately, I have my father to help me look after it. Seeing you juggle all this alone and still standing strong and confident to face the consequences is what I love about you. I want this strong and confident Taani, not a normal wife. Now, coming to your other worry of hitting the bed and falling asleep immediately because you get exhausted daily by your work routine is not even a problem. I want to be there for you when you hit the pillow so I can cuddle you while you sleep in my arms. So, I can kiss your forehead every night and hear you murmur my name as I make sweet love to you. Trust me, Taani, the nights when you are too spent to even think about me, I won't mind sleeping in another room and letting you have your personal space."

"Sameer," a soft gasp escapes her lips as she processes my words, but I don't let her speak and continue to share my thoughts with her.

"Taani, that's what couples do. They share responsibilities between them. I don't just want your ups in life. I want to be there for you in both your ups and downs. Especially the downs because I know you'll always need someone to cuddle you when you are at your lowest."

A tear falls from her eye as she cups my face, grinning.

"Please, marry me, Sameer," she requests, and my breath catches in my throat for a moment. I keep my expressions neutral, even though my heart is jumping inside.

I think I am hallucinating when she pulls my face closer, stands between my legs, and pushes me towards the table until I lean on it. "Say, yes, Sameer Khanna, before I change my mind."

She looks dead serious, her eyes boring into mine, urging me to accept her proposal. She runs a thumb over my bottom lip, and her eyes follow her hand movement as though waiting for me to open my mouth.

"Yes."

As soon as I agree to her proposal, Taani blushes and licks her lips. My gaze latches on her lush glistening lips, but before I can make a move, Taani leans forward and claims my lips. I love it when she shows her bossy nature by taking what is hers and is not afraid to show it. Just thinking about my marriage to Taani makes the blood rush to my manhood, which is aching in dire need for this woman.

Her kiss is filled with a ferocious hunger like she wants to own me completely with just her lips. I clutch her ponytail at the back of her head, drag her mouth closer to mine and kiss her back with equal hunger, our tongues dancing in perfect harmony. I'm sure she can feel my desire for her, through this one kiss. Circling her waist, I draw her to me as we part to take a breath.

My free hand slides up the silky-smooth skin of her arms while her fingers keep slipping into my hair as though loving the feel of them. With every move, Taani shivers as I stroke her collar bone before placing an open-mouthed kiss. She's soft everywhere, and I can't get a grip on my fingers, nor does she try to stop me.

"When you get the time, make a list of all your pending wishes," I tell and place another kiss on her neck.
Taani pulls my head to look into my eyes. "Why?"

I stroke her lips, murmuring.
"You gave me a beautiful gift by agreeing to marry me because I fulfilled your five wishes. You are very generous, Taani. So, if I complete all your wishes, maybe, you'll finally give me all of you, body and soul."
She looks outrageously sexy as she ponders over the meaning behind my words and kisses me again,

slow and tender. Heat radiates through our bodies as we kiss each other again and again until her intercom rings.

"Our fifteen minutes is up." She groans in displeasure and quickly puts some distance between us. I think the crazy spell is broken as Taani switches back to her work mode.

Remorse fills her expression on our interruption.
"Go, crack some deals while I call my parents and tell them to fly to India immediately."

Taani frowns, a bit nervous, but I know she is happy.
"I want to get engaged and marry you as soon as possible.
I don't want a long gap between the two. We can know each other's strengths and weaknesses after marriage. I can't wait too long to make you mine," I mention, only to be interrupted by the intercom again, annoying us both.

"I should go." She mutters.
"So should I," I kiss her forehead before making my way to the door happily because now that she has agreed to marry me, I have nothing to lose.
Before I turn the doorknob, Taani reaches me and turns me around. She then wipes something from the corner of my lips, which I assume is her lipstick mark. I immediately stop her from continuing.
"Don't wipe it off. I liked the taste of it."
Her cheeks turn tomato red at my remark, but she is very sharp in responding to my teasing.
"I'll gift you my lip gloss then. Keep licking it if you love the taste so much. But for now, I don't want my

staff to know what happened here. It's quite unprofessional."

I chuckle as she completes her task and gives my face a once-over to see if anything is left.

"Now, you may go."

"Hmm," I agree. "Since you are so conscious, I would suggest you do a touchup yourself before heading for your next meeting. Anyone can read it on your face that you just kissed the most handsome man in town."

She tries to cover her face to hide the red staining her cheeks, but she can't hide it from me. I love to see her blush. Taani opens the door for me.

"Don't act smart, Mr. Khanna. I have seen hotter men than you."

"Sure you have," I pin her to the door. "But you haven't kissed them; you kissed me. That makes me special, and I can't thank you enough for making it so memorable, Miss Gupta."

I kiss her cheek, the sound reverberating in the silence of the cabin. I then pull away from her and let myself out, grinning like an idiot. I seriously cannot believe what just happened. I came to her office thinking about the endless possibilities of Taani denying the attraction and feelings we have for each other. But now, I am leaving this place with memories I'll always cherish. I am already feeling on top of the world.

As soon as I reach home, I call my parents to give them the news, and they are equally happy that Taani agreed to marry me. My dad calls his assistant to book them on the weekend flight while talking to me over a video call. He is excited for me. And Mom is already making plans to call up the priest and speak to Vansh's grandmother to select the best date for the engagement and wedding.

I can't sleep at night and keep on remembering our chat in her office today. I recall how Taani expressed her fears that she might never be a typical wife for me, how I put those fears to rest, her sudden proposal asking me to marry her and our kiss. Damn! My body heated up on remembering her lips on mine, and now I was aching badly for her again. I quickly pick up my phone to message Taani, but suddenly I remember she must have reached home exhausted after the client party she attended today and must be asleep now. Her hectic schedule will not leave any room for us to text, call and have romantic talks at night as other couples do. But I don't mind. I am getting the woman I desire. I don't need anything else. I am in no hurry apart from having her by my side as my lawfully wedded wife.

Taani

Two weeks Later

Sameer and I got engaged one week ago at the VK mansion, where a lot of drama unfolded, and Vansh and Vidhi confessed that they were already married. But since Vansh's family wasn't a part of their marriage, five years ago, the Kapoors decided to get them married again along with Sameer and me. So now, after two weeks, both of us sisters will be tying the knot with our respective partners. It felt like a dream. Marriage was not in my cards anytime soon, and definitely not when I was looking for grooms for my sister. And now that I am engaged to Sameer, wearing his ring on my finger, I can already see how my life will be changing soon. I met Sameer's parents for the first time during our engagement, though I had already spoken to them many times before that. They are a sweet couple, and now that I am officially engaged to their son, I am thrilled to have a family of my own. A father to pamper me, a mother to give me the affection I always craved, and a husband, who I know will love me unconditionally.

While these thoughts of being a part of a full-fledged family were exciting, they also scared me. I wondered if I would be able to do justice to them. I had excess on my plate in terms of my work that even taking out a week for my honeymoon sounded difficult. But Sameer made it look so easy. He suggested I carry my laptop to Bali, where we four, Sameer and I, Vidhi and Vansh, were going on a honeymoon. It was Vidhi's idea to go together, and I wonder how Vansh agreed to it. As far as I have seen them, he was always desperate to spend time with her alone, whenever and wherever possible, while Sameer and I were still learning the ropes and trying to take it slow. Sameer had shown immense patience regarding my work schedule and had respected my wish to not jump into physical intimacy until we knew each other completely. We hardly spent time together, and I take the blame for it, but Sameer never complained, nor did he hurry to make me his. Daadi was right. I really couldn't have gotten a better partner than Sameer Khanna. I was lucky enough to grab him and make him mine.

In the last two weeks, Sameer and I have kissed a lot, but that was all I was comfortable with at the moment, and he never crossed the line, even when I could sense his desire to do more every time we were together.

"Ma'am, the Khanna family is here."

My maid's voice breaks my trance. Today, I have invited Sameer and his parents to the Gupta villa for dinner. I wanted Vidhi here tonight to host them with me, but she is busy with Vansh's family, who is thrilled to have her as their daughter-in-law. I couldn't have asked for a better family for my sister, and I felt a sense of satisfaction at having fulfilled my promise to Vidhi's mother.

I was in the kitchen instructing the chefs to arrange everything on the dining table, and now that I know the Khannas are here, I can't wait to meet them. Sameer has been to my home a few times after we got engaged, but only to drop me from the office or the parties I had to attend. That was the only time we could spend with each other during the ride back home since he knew my energy was always drained by the end of the day.

As I come out of the kitchen, Sameer's eyes light up as he sees me in a dark blue dress that he gifted me and wanted me to wear tonight. It's a beautiful silk dress resting above my knees, and though I was a bit hesitant to wear it in front of his parents, he urged me that I should.

"Hello, Aunty, hello, Uncle," I greet his parents and bend down to take their blessings, but they both stop me before I touch their feet and hug me instead.

"Still uncle and aunty?" his mother frowns.

"Mom," Sameer chides. "Didn't we discuss this already?"

She nods and smiles, cupping my face. I have no clue what discussion they had on this topic, but it looked like Sameer had convinced his parents not to force me to address them as Mom and Dad as he did, until I was ready in my heart.

"Take your time, sweetheart," she kisses my forehead. "We are so happy to have a daughter in our family, and we are fine with whatever you call us."

"Did Sameer tell you not to force me regarding this?" I inquire, and though his Mom is confused if she should reply, his father does.

"Sameer has warned us not to do anything that can spoil your mood. So, you see how much he threatens us to ensure we don't confuse or upset you."

I glare at Sameer, who gives me a coy smile.

"They are just exaggerating, Taani. I didn't threaten them at all."

"And dare you do, Sameer," I snap. "They are my in-laws, and I won't tolerate my fiancé scaring them off."

His parents laugh heartily at seeing me scold Sameer, and soon I join them, whereas Sameer Khanna stands there looking sheepish and utterly cute.

After showing them the house, I leave them in the living room again to ensure my chefs and staff have arranged everything in the dining room.

"The curries will be at the centre, Rita," I tell my staff as she has placed them incorrectly. "And don't forget to serve the Gulab jamuns to Sameer's father. He loves it."

"Yes, Ma'am." Rita nods and goes back to the kitchen for further preparations, and just when I am about to turn, a pair of strong arms hug me from behind.

"Sameer?" I gasp.

"What about my favourite dessert?" he teases, kissing my earlobe.

God! This man is always touchy and needy. And he is turning me just like him. I am getting addicted to his touch.

"Why do you need another dessert when you have me?" I tease back.

Emboldened by my words, Sameer grinds his pelvis against mine, and a moan escapes my lips.

"I can't wait to taste my favourite dessert then," he whispers in my ears in his ever-so sexy voice.

"Can I come in?" Sameer's mother clears her throat, bringing us back to reality. I instantly push Sameer away and turn around to face his mother, who is grinning at us.

Sameer is as disoriented as I am, knowing his mother saw us in the middle of our romance.

"Aunty, please come in."

Sameer brushes his fingers in his hair before smiling at his mother.

"I'll give Dad company," he gives an excuse and marches out before Aunty can tease us back.

"The food will be served in ten minutes, Aunty. I hope that's not a problem." I tell her.

"Not at all, Taani. And you don't have to be so formal with us. I love how wonderful a hostess you are, though. And the aroma of the food is making my mouth water. I am so lucky to get a daughter-in-law like you, who excels at everything she does."

My face drops at her remark.

"Aunty, I...I didn't cook all this. I mean, I hardly get time to cook, so I never..." I pause again, feeling mortified. "The chefs cooked the meals tonight as I am not an expert in cooking."

Seeing my hesitation, Sameer's mother pats my cheek.

"Who said I expected you to be an expert cook? I am not the typical mother-in-law that you see on television. I already guessed your chefs cooked the meal tonight, and there is nothing wrong with that. But let me take pride in telling you that Sameer is a great cook. He will pamper you by cooking delicious meals every day, and you won't be able to resist."

I am surprised at her forward thinking. She is the first woman I have heard or met so far who is okay with her son doing the chores, which are generally expected from a woman. As though reading my thoughts, Sameer's mother smiles warmly at me.

"I have raised a man who believes in equality, Taani. He is unlike the other men who want their wives to do everything for them. He believes in returning the favour too. In fact, I assure you he will always be prepared to take up equal responsibilities in your married life, like taking care of household duties. He might be the broody CEO when working with his father, but at home, he is the best son, who wants his mother to rest and wouldn't mind cooking for the family on weekends. I am so proud of him, and one day, you will be too. I am sure of that."

I am so pleased to learn about this side of Sameer, which obviously he would never tell me himself. Thanks to his mother, the last shreds of self-doubt have disappeared, and now I can confidently say I am marrying the right man.

The dinner is served, and Sameer sits next to me while his parents take the opposite end. We are all discussing the upcoming wedding preparation, which was to happen in two weeks, when Sameer gently puts his hands on the silk dress over my thigh and caresses it. Acting casual, I glare at him to stop doing that, but he pretends to be oblivious to what he is doing to me below the table and continues to talk to his parents, telling them about our honeymoon plans in Bali with Vansh-Vidhi. I gasp when his fingers ride up the hem of my dress and, pulling it upwards, stroke my inner thighs.

I quickly pick up my phone and type a message.

'Is that why you asked me to wear this dress tonight? So that you get enough access?'

I hit send, and Sameer's phone vibrates. He takes it out from his suit pocket, reads it and types back a reply, holding his phone below the table so that his parents don't realize we are texting each other in their presence.

'Yes. Besides, it's been 54 hours since I touched you properly.'
I grin, reading his reply but still give a disapproving stare. Sameer's brow shoots up, and he tries to move his hand away, thinking I don't like it, but I shock him by holding his wrist and putting his palm back on my exposed thigh. A gasp escapes his lips, and when I look at his face, I see a dark hunger in his eyes, which makes me clench my thighs together to subside the sudden ache that's starting to take hold of my body.

Sameer thankfully doesn't touch me beyond that, and his fingers keep skimming the skin of my thighs to his heart's content. If only he knew what his touch was doing to me, if only he knew how his touch was enough for the tingle between my legs to grow stronger and more demanding.

Once we were done with dinner, Sameer insisted I show him my bedroom, and I once again am a bit mortified that he requested that in front of his parents, who didn't seem to mind. They ask us to go ahead while they check out the little plant nursery in my garden. I had heard from Sameer that his parents are fond of gardening. So, the moment they are gone, I lead Sameer to my bedroom.

"So, this is where we will live." He declares happily, glancing around the room and the décor.
Yes! This is where we will live after marriage until Sameer and I decide how to manage the living arrangements with our businesses in two different

countries. We were yet to figure that out, and for a few weeks after our marriage, Sameer will be staying with me in Gupta Villa while his parents leave for London. His father will take care of his office while Sameer will work online from here and take care of the rest.

"You can tell me your preferences for this room, and I'll arrange it accordingly."
Since Sameer will be staying in this room with me, I want him to be comfortable.

"Isn't your bed too big?" he mocks, and I am about to agree blankly. But then I realize he is just teasing me. "I am serious, Taani. Isn't your bed too big? It'll only be us sleeping on it, not a whole army. Let's get a smaller bed to cozy against each other."

"You never leave a chance to flirt, do you?"

He laughs at my question and pulls me in his arms again.

"The room is perfect because it's yours, and when I say I want you, I want everything that you have in your life, the way it is, without any changes, including the bed. It's fine, even if it's gigantic. We will make our memories on it. As it is, half of it is going to remain unused." He winks at me, and I again blush, realizing the naughty innuendo.

But I am seriously impressed. Where does he find such charming words to woo me every single time?
"Sameer, are you sure?" I ask him again.
"I should be asking you that," he teases. "Are you sure you'll not kick me out of the bedroom every day

because I snore and that might disturb your beauty sleep?”

I hit his chest gently.

“Stop joking. I’m talking about your work arrangements after marriage. Are you sure you will stay with me until we find a solution? Won’t you miss your parents? I don’t want them to think I am taking advantage of you.”

“You know what?” He interrupts as a mischievous grin plays on his lips. “I don’t mind if you take advantage of me.”

“Gosh, Sameer, I am serious,” I try to push him away, blushing again. This is becoming a regular occurrence.

“Taani.” Sameer pulls me to him again and cups my cheeks.

“I’ll miss my parents and vice versa, but they understand that by marrying you, I’ll have some responsibilities towards our relationship too. I am not leaving this place until we find a middle ground regarding our work issues.”

I am thrilled by his resolve. Sameer is truly being a wonderful partner and is filling in for me where I could fall short in the future. The mere thought of it makes me love him even more. How did I manage to survive all these years without Sameer? Only if I had known my soulmate existed somewhere in this world who would prioritize me above everything else, I would have crossed mountains to bring Sameer sooner into my life. But never mind, our *Love by Chance* is finally on track.

CHAPTER 10

Sameer

Finally, D-Day arrived. Taani and I took the seven pheras before the holy fire, promising to always be there for each other till eternity, in the good and bad times. Vidhi and Vansh also exchanged vows on the same day as us. Therefore, being a twin wedding, the event wasn't a private affair anymore. The Kapoors and my parents made it a grand celebration and invited everyone from our family and business circle to be a part of our happiness and shower blessings upon us. Vansh's grandmother, a traditional woman at heart, insisted on completing all the pre-wedding rituals for us, and we both couples had lots of fun and entertainment throughout the ceremonies.

At last, the wedding rituals are over, and Taani is surrounded by a bevy of elderly ladies from my family. I can't help but be curious about their talks and go near them to listen in on their conversation. They are grilling Taani on how she would manage to run her business and married life together. A few even asked her how soon we were planning a baby.

Just as I am about to rescue Taani, Mom reaches her and takes her away, saving her from further embarrassment. I am worried that this whole incident will bring Taani's self-doubt—about her giving equal priority to work and home—to the fore again.

At night, after evading my relatives and letting my parents take care of the guests, I finally enter Taani's bedroom, which we will be sharing from now on. I see her pacing in the room in the same bridal lehenga she wore today. She hasn't changed her dress nor removed the heavy jewellery from her body and is murmuring something to herself. I take a moment to admire this woman, who is now my wife. It all seems like a dream. Taani and I met by chance at a conference, and from that day onwards, she had my heart. Tonight, seeing her all decked up for me, wearing the traditional sindoor (vermillion) and Mangalsutra (marital chain), made me realize that finally, Taani was mine, and mine alone.

"Sameer," Taani's voice breaks my trance. She rushes toward me, and I meet her halfway in the room. The moment she reaches me, she begins to rant. "I can't do this. I...I really can't be the way your family wants me to be. One of your aunts told me maintaining a long-distance affair is far easier than holding on to a long-distance marriage. She is confident this marriage won't last. And your other aunt, who came from Jaipur, thinks we should plan a baby soon since your parents are fond of kids and want to see their grandchildren soon. And-"

I grab her arms. I knew she would get upset by the relatives hounding her, giving her all sorts of advice, but I never thought she would get this rattled.

"Taani, relax."

"No, Sameer. There's more. I-"

"Shh," I hush her, and take her straight to the dressing mirror and make her sit on the chair.

"Sameer, I don't think I can ever fulfill their expectations."

"You don't have to." I kneel before her and help her take off the heavy bangles she's been wearing. "None of those expectations matter to me, Taani. It's their perspective, their opinion. They don't know what we have between us, nor will they understand."

Her anxiety subsides as she listens to me intently. I keep taking off her bangles and then go for the heavy pair of anklets she's wearing. All this jewellery belonged to her mother, and it was Taani's wish to wear them at our wedding, even though they looked old-fashioned. The emotions attached to them were more important to us, and that's all that mattered.

"It's time you stop paying attention to what others think about our future. They are not the ones who are going to build it, but us."

I take off her anklets and put them on the dressing table. Taani is relaxed now. The moment I slide my hand to the back of her neck to unhook the necklace, Taani stops me.

"I ruined it, didn't I?" she asks remorsefully. "In my anxious state, I didn't follow the first rule that is a must for every bride during her wedding night."

First rule? What is she talking about? Taani looks at the frown on my face and continues to explain.

"I was told to sit on the bed all decked up for you. And instead, I vented out all my apprehensions about our future, that too, when we just took vows to be together forever. I am already proving to be a bad wife."

"Thank God you didn't sit like that, covering your face with your bridal veil. That would have been a total cliché, Taani. C'mon. Don't you see? From the time we met, have we ever followed the norms? And I still don't get the concept of the groom unveiling his wife on the wedding night when he already knows how she looks. I mean, there is no surprise element, is there?"

I want to cheer her, but Taani is still dejected despite my many attempts to make her smile. So, I cup her face and pull her to me.

"Look at me, Taani," I urge her to meet my eyes. "Do you see any regret on my face for marrying you? This is the best day of my life, and it doesn't matter if you weren't on the bed on our wedding night when I stepped into the room. Just clear all these thoughts from your mind. You look exhausted and definitely in need of some sleep. C'mon. Let's go to sleep."

I get up and lead her to the walk-in closet.

"Go, get changed and then we are hitting the bed. Just tell me which side you usually sleep on, so I'll take the other one."

Taani smiles at my attempt to divert her mind.

"I always sleep on the left," she murmurs.

"I'll take the right side of the bed then." I wink at her and I begin to unbutton my sherwani. Her eyes widen in surprise, and shyness takes hold of her, making her blush like a tomato. She hesitates and is about to say something before she turns and goes to the bathroom.

Half an hour later, we are both on the bed, facing each other, with an arm-distance space between us, though our fingers are entwined. Taani is wearing a lavender-coloured silk night suit, whereas I am only in my night pants. There's a heavy silence floating around us, and we haven't stopped gazing at each other.
"I am not trying to seduce you by not wearing a T-shirt. I like to sleep without it." I mention this to Taani, who has her eyes on my face. She is hesitant to drop her gaze below that.

A smile creeps on her face at my remark.

"Sameer Khanna...always a gentleman," she whispers, pressing our hands tight. "You know what I was thinking?"

How would I know what she was thinking? I am still trying to process that finally, Taani is my wife, and I am on her bed, sleeping close to her.

"It feels like a dream, Sameer. I, Taani Gupta, married. It all feels so surreal. Marriage was never on my cards anytime soon."

The moment she says this, I lean over and touch her luscious lips, feeling the sweetness of her lips on mine but do not attempt to kiss her.

"Now, do you believe we are married?" I ask, my heart drumming a crazy beat to know her reply.
Taani licks her lips.
"I only believe you 20%," she murmurs coyly.
I lean over her face, kissing her again, taking my own sweet
time to suck on her lower lip and just when she parts her lips, I pull away.

"Now?"
I don't know who is panting between us, or is it both?
"50%."
She is in a mood to play this game, and it gives me a sense of joy to know she wants me to continue.
Our mouths latch on to the other once again. Taani's fingers play with my hair, tugging them hard while I hungrily feel her up and weigh her soft breasts in my palms.

"Now?" I gasp against her neck, squeezing the delicate and soft mounds with my hands.
"Seventy," she mutters, totally disoriented by my slow torture.

We kiss again, deep and hot, yet impossibly tender. None of us realizes the position we are in, Taani is pinned beneath me, and I am above her, settled perfectly between her legs. I move my mouth from her lips to her neck, scraping my jaw to the sensitive skin behind her ear.

"Now?"
"Ninety," she replies. Her voice is a throaty whisper, devoid of control.
My lower body shudders with arousal as Taani rubs her body vigorously against mine to feel my weight.

She grinds her body against my hardness in desperation, something I have never seen doing before.

"Taani," I whisper, gazing at her flushed face and her aroused body, waiting to be touched by me. She opens her eyes to meet mine. "Are you ready for more?"

I am yearning to make her mine, and I hope she wants the same. As soon as she opens her mouth to respond, her phone rings on the bedside table. Who the hell is calling her on our wedding night? The spell is broken, and the haze of desire is gone from her eyes as she slowly wriggles beneath me. I shift to my side of the bed to allow her to answer the call.

"Take the call," I rein in my desire. "Maybe it's important."

She gives me a nervous smile before answering. It's her assistant, Pooja. As Taani speaks to her, I realize they are talking about some client escalation which needs Taani's intervention to respond to an urgent email. If she doesn't, it could hamper her business truce with the client. She quickly gets down from the bed, opens her laptop on her work table and looks at me with a guilt-ridden face.

"Give me 20 minutes, Sameer."

I nod in affirmation, though I don't know how I'll sleep on this bed without her for even twenty seconds. I watch her log in to her laptop, and she is engrossed in her work. Without glancing at me even once, Taani continues to work like tonight is just another night of her life. We were married today, and she's working, leaving me on the bed, craving for her. But there is no point in overthinking. I have signed up for this; to allow her work to be her top priority above everything else, including me. I know the day will come when she'll have all her time for me and me only. I pray hard for that day to come sooner rather than later.

Taani

"Taani?"

I hear Sameer's voice waking me gently. I stir to find my neck hurting badly. I open my eyes to Sameer's sexy face. The room is still dark, and the only light is the lamp on my study table, where I dozed off after emailing my client. That's the reason my neck is aching. When did I fall asleep? What time is it? Sameer has already shut my laptop.

"Let's get you to bed." Sameer leans down, and before I can tell him anything, he carries me in his arms. I am such an idiot. It was my wedding night, and instead of being in Sameer's arms on the bed, I spent half of the night working. But this email was really urgent, and I couldn't push it to tomorrow morning. I slide my arms around Sameer's neck as he effortlessly carries me and gently places me on the bed. It's 4:00 a.m. as I check the bedside table clock. Sameer takes his side on the bed after covering me with the duvet, and I feel guilty as hell for being such an inattentive wife.

As soon as he joins me on the bed, I try to kiss him, and though he kisses me back, he doesn't initiate further intimacy. Sameer strokes my head.

"You need to sleep, Taani. Work has drained all your energy already. Get some rest." He pecks my forehead.

I like his sensibilities and the way he always puts my needs before his. I cuddle him. Being wrapped in his incredible cocoon, I can feel his body heat all over me, smell his skin and touch his bare back and chest. I place my head in the crook of his neck while his arm wraps around my hip, giving me intense pleasure. Being married feels heavenly. Or rather, being married to Sameer Khanna feels heavenly.

****

I once again wake up to the sight of Sameer clad in a towel covering his lower half. It's morning, and it looks like he's just showered and is brushing his hair before my dressing mirror. Having to share my room with someone else is new to me, but Sameer is my husband, and he is as particular about keeping things orderly as I am, so, fortunately, that's a relief. I blink hazily as his arms flex, revealing his biceps as Sameer rakes his hair with his hands while applying the gel. He hasn't realized I am awake. That gives me a chance to ogle him the way I want to. I can't believe this handsome specimen is mine. My gaze slides through the deep arches of his bare back that gives his body symmetry, and I stop as I reach the hem of his towel. I can see his boxers peeking out of the towel and can read the brand name, Calvin Klein. The man sure has good taste in his undergarments. He has a taut butt and strong thigh muscles. I feel an unsettling sensation in my core, a hunger taking hold of me whenever I look at Sameer.

Hold on! What time is it? And why didn't my alarms ring? It looks quite sunny, as though it's past 09:00. I check the bedside clock and realize it's 10:30 a.m.

"What?" I scream as I push the duvet aside to check my phone.

That brings Sameer's attention to me, who suddenly gives me a startled look.

"Jeez…you scared the hell out of me," Sameer screams in equal horror.

The knot on his towel loosens and, in slow motion, drops off his body, revealing the exact colour and shape of his boxers, and my gaze automatically drops to the tent that forms in his boxers. I have never seen a man in an aroused state before. Sameer clad only in his boxers is a vision I can behold forever in my naughty mind. Sameer follows my line of vision, but my eyes defy me as they refuse to look away from his bulging member.

With measured steps, Sameer reaches the edge of the bed, and my heart beats erratically when he stands between my legs.
"I never thought my newly wedded wife would scare me like this in the morning."

He pulls my chin up to meet his eyes.

"Good morning, Taani. Your morning look is unimaginably gorgeous," he murmurs, stroking the corner of my lips with his thumb.
I try my best to compose myself and not give in to what is happening between us right now.

"Why didn't you wake me up? I never get up so late, and why didn't my alarms ring?"
"I didn't wake you up because you slept late. It's okay to oversleep sometimes, especially when you are not working, and I turned off your alarms as I had promised you once."

He turned them off? Before I can argue, Sameer leans over me and in an attempt to put some distance between us, I shuffle myself, and my knuckles accidentally graze the bulge in his boxers. Is it hard or semi-hard? I don't know. I have never touched a man's privates before, nor did I want to, until now. My cheeks burn on imagining what it would feel like to touch him without the barrier of this soft fabric between us, and again the ache between my legs intensifies.

"Sameer, wear something, please." I stutter. I don't think my heart and eyes want him to dress up, but his near-nakedness is making me jittery. I can see him like this forever. Clothes don't do justice to his sexy body at all.

"First, I am going to punish you for scaring me and my towel," he winks.

My chest rises and falls with every breath as Sameer leans over me, making me fall back on the bed, and I know he is going to kiss me. I soon get up, balance myself on my elbows and press my palms over his chest, grazing his taut buds. The moment my hand slides over his bud, Sameer groans softly, a sound which is new to me but exciting enough to feel tingly all over my body.
"Sameer, I am already late." I remind him.

"One kiss," he urges, his raw desire evident as Sameer lays me on the bed and hovers above me, about to kiss me.

I didn't know marriage came with this craving, a feeling so edgy that it makes you lose control of your body and give in to your desires, none of which I ever thought I would experience myself.

I squeeze my eyes shut, letting him take control, but the next moment Sameer roves his hand downwards from the top of my body, making my breath hitch. He rests his hands on my belly button and starts to tickle my stomach. I laugh hysterically, moving from side to side at his sweet assault on my body. I thought he would kiss me, but he chose to be naughty instead. Sameer knows I am not yet comfortable with physical intimacy, and he respected my wishes, creating a diversion.

We roll on the bed such that I find myself straddling him. I can feel his hardness between my legs and try to ignore the feelings that invade my body because I know if I give in, we'll end up doing something which I want to take time to cherish.

Sameer observes me intently as I lean over his chest, breathing his musky cologne. I have never seen Sameer clean-shaven, and I love how he impeccably grooms his French beard. He trims it just the way I like it, rough on the edges.

Sameer pulls me closer to kiss me, and though I want this kiss as much as he does, I want to tease him as it's payback time. So, when his lips brush over mine,

I nip him on the neck, careful to not leave a mark and push him to the other side of the bed.

Before he catches me, I run to the bathroom.

"Taani? Come here." Sameer grunts and I give him a cheeky smile.
"That's payback for shutting off my alarms. Never do that again Mr. Khanna, or else this is what you'll get from me, and that's … no intimacy."

He reaches the bathroom door before I can close it and tries to drag me out again, making me laugh.

"Okay, okay. Fine. Let's compensate for this with a quick shower together. How does that sound?" I ask.

Sameer's eyes widen with a dark hunger.

"You mean it?" He's already breathing hard.
"Very much," I whisper, and just when he closes the gap between us to kiss me, I nip the other side of his neck, harder this time, so as to leave a mark and run to the bathroom, shutting the door on time.
"Taani, what the hell has gotten into you?" Sameer shouts, banging the door. "You bit me twice."
"You thought you were marrying a kitten, didn't you, Sameer? I am wild and untamed, just in case you haven't realized it yet."

I hear his laughter from the other side of the door, which makes me smile. It's obvious Sameer will not let me get out of the bedroom without a kiss so easily, but I love to challenge him and to see him yearn for me.

****

It's three days to our marriage, and Sameer's parents are ready to fly back to London as his father has to handle the business there. Though Sameer's mom wanted to stay back with us, she couldn't leave her husband alone to manage everything in their London house.

"He didn't even let me stay at my parent's house for more than a day when we were newly married. And that still hasn't changed. Sameer's father can't function without me. He needs me around all the time. That's why I made sure these traits don't pass on to my son. I wanted Sameer to let his wife be independent on her terms."

I smile at his mom, glancing quickly at Sameer, who hugs his father. We are at the airport to see them off, and in the evening, we are also flying to Bali with Vansh and Vidhi for our honeymoon.

"Take care of yourself and enjoy your honeymoon," she adds, kissing my forehead.

I take her blessings, and as they depart toward the gates, my eyes well with tears. I'll miss them. Even if we didn't get much time to spend together, they filled the void of my parents, pampering me with love, something I had missed for a long time in my life. Sameer hugs me on seeing me cry. In these three days of our marriage, I have worked till late, and Sameer had been patient enough to let me do so. At times, he was the one who carried me to bed as I dozed off before the laptop. And not even once has he shown impatience and hurry to consummate our marriage. He wants me to come to him ready for this most important moment in our life. It's not that I don't crave this physical intimacy with Sameer. I really do, a lot more than I show it to him, but I want to take this slow. I have always been an introvert and have had only a few close friends so far. Trusting new people has always been difficult for me. Entering into this relationship is a risk I have taken in my life. So, to entrust him completely with my body and soul will take some time from my side. I trust Sameer, but I don't want to lose my control over the hormones right now because, at present, I am already facing a lot of hits concerning a major client deal my company has been trying to crack for a long time. A little distraction on my part and I can lose this deal, which my Dad wanted in our kitty for a long time. Once I am done with this, I promise to give all my attention to Sameer and my wifely duties towards him. It could take a few months—maybe four to five if I am right.

CHAPTER 11

Taani

Bali – Honeymoon

This is bliss. Since I took over my father's company, I have never had a holiday. I have travelled the world, but only for my business and never for pleasure. Even though I am working at night, Sameer and I have spent enough time together dancing, drinking, swimming, strolling around this little island and experiencing thrilling water rides. Our villa is beautiful with panoramic vistas of the ocean and has a private infinity pool. The floating breakfast is something that I look forward to eagerly every morning, not because the breakfast is yummy, but because my husband serves me in his hot avatar, sexy swimming trunks with water droplets glistening on his Adonis-like body. Earlier I used to hesitate to ogle him openly, but now I do that a lot, blatantly, and Sameer is just waiting for me to take this admiration further and show him in action. As we have breakfast together in the pool, I roam my gaze hungrily over his wet body, and Sameer notices it immediately.

"The chocolate sauce is dripping on your neck, Taani."
Sameer's voice breaks my stupor. We are both in the pool, with me in a blue bikini, exposing a good amount of cleavage. I recently bought this bikini as blue is Sameer's favourite colour, and I had reserved wearing such revealing outfits for private occasions. I am moody these days, especially when Sameer is so close to me, and it hurts me to see him aching in pain for not being able to have the honeymoon of his dreams.

"Where? Here?" I ask him as I dab a tissue over my neckline.

Sameer moves the breakfast basket away before walking toward me in the water. Just as I think he will take that tissue from me and dab it where the sauce is, Sameer leans forward and licks it off my neck. That one swipe of his tongue is enough for me to buck my hips and grab his arms for support. He pulls away to lick his lips, which still have chocolate on them and looks intensely into my eyes. Before he can lick them off completely, I grab his face and touch my lips to his, licking him off. He tastes like sin with the chocolate smeared on his lips, and I'd be lying if I said I don't want him. Sameer pushes me to the edge of the pool, kissing me feverishly, taking his own sweet time to suck on my lower lip. Our hunger for food is long forgotten and is replaced with an uncontrollable desire to satiate the hunger of our bodies and our soul.

Every night I slept in Sameer's arms—we would kiss and touch each other too, but never beyond my permission, and that made him the most adorable husband ever. Today, I wanted him to blur a few lines and take a step further toward our intimacy. Sameer sinks his teeth into my bare shoulder. More than him, I craved his touch, and today for the first time, I want him to love me a bit more than usual. When I push myself into his manly body, feeling up his arms, chest and his wet back with my fingers, Sameer takes the hint to continue.

Holding me by the waist, he raises me and makes me sit on the edge of the pool. He kisses me all over my body through my bikini. I slide out of the pool and lie down on my back, with Sameer hovering over me and kissing me everywhere. His wet tongue traces the shape of my ear. He licks the pulse below my ear softly, making me shiver, before trailing a tingling path along my neck. His mesmerizing lips move downwards, touching my tender breasts which are aching for him. Sameer slides my bikini off my upper body, exposing my breasts to his naked eyes. He has never removed my clothes before, but isn't that what I wanted from him today? To blur a few lines of restraint that I have drawn between us? I watch him stare at my mounds hungrily before feasting over them, and everything else becomes a blur to me. I let the pleasure seep into every pore of my skin which has started to erupt in goosebumps wherever Sameer is touching and devouring me. I can't believe we are doing this in broad daylight, that too, by the pool. But that's what a honeymoon is all about, right? It never goes as planned.

My breath hitches as his lips create a hot pattern over

my stomach, and he lowers himself and sucks my naval. I can literally see everything, from rainbows to stars, in broad daylight. I knew with Sameer pleasuring me, I would feel cherished and loved. But everything comes to a halt when his lips move lower, and his fingers trace my tiny fabric below. That's when I grab his wrists.

Sameer stops immediately, and I open my squeezed eyes to look down at him. A loud groan passes through his lips as he reaches above and looks into my eyes.
"I am sorry, Taani," he swallows remorsefully. "I know you want to take things slow, and I'm completely with you on it."
He kisses my forehead lovingly and looks at me again. I stare up at his handsome face and palm his cheek.
"At times, I feel I am really taking advantage of you, Sameer. You don't deserve this."

Sameer frowns and bites my cheek.
"Awww." I yelp in pain.

"Say that again, and I am biting you everywhere. Don't you ever say that I don't deserve you. I know we had an arranged marriage, and you didn't get enough time to know me properly. You are not the kind of woman who gives in to their bodily desires and consummates their marriage just for the sake of it. I know you want to fall in love with me before you give me that right on you, and I can wait. Because claiming your body after owning your heart is what I want too. So, it's okay. We will go at your pace, and this is good. It's not that you are keeping me entirely at bay. We have our moments, and we will have many more of them. And trust me, Mrs. Taani Sameer Khanna, you'll beg me one day to make love to you. And I will be right here, waiting for you when that day arrives."

He nips my nose softly, making me smile. He already has a major chunk of my heart, and now after his intense declaration, I know, for a fact, that I am beginning to fall in love with my husband.

Sameer gets off me and pulls a white Turkish robe from the lounger. I shyly cover my upper body, and Sameer helps me wear the robe. I know what control it takes for a man to come so close to worshipping his woman and stop. He kisses my forehead again.
"I'll be back in a moment, and then we are finishing that breakfast."
I know he has gone to the washroom to take care of that hard bulge inside his swimming trunks. I stare at his retreating back, thinking if God is still creating men like Sameer Khanna. I don't think he does anymore because my Sameer is one of a kind.

Sameer

It effing hurts me that Taani is still keeping her distance from me. Yes, as a husband, I can understand her, but the crazy lover in me is going insane every time she lets me worship her body. I really want to give her the world, but she only does what she wants. Taani is a woman with admirable clarity about what she wants out of life. I haven't met anyone like her ever. She is a level-headed woman with iron control, who doesn't indulge and give in to her temporary desires, and that is what has made me want her as my partner in the first place.

It's been almost three weeks since we were back from our honeymoon, and even though, unlike most couples, we might not have united in terms of our bodies, we were still getting closer, bonding with each other and being comfortable with each other. I'm taking care of my business from India for the moment. Dad and Mom have been extremely supportive of my decision to let Taani set her own pace until we decide how to find a middle ground regarding our marital lives without affecting our respective businesses. So far, we haven't reached any decision, but I am sure we will find one very soon.

"I am home," Taani shouts from the living room. Tonight, she was home late as she had to attend an after-work event. As soon as I hear her voice, I ask the chefs to arrange our dinner.

"Welcome, baby," I reach outside, and in no time, she is in my arms, and we are kissing.

One thing we have never stopped doing since we got married is kissing the hell out of each other when she leaves for the office and when she returns home. The first kiss is to help us both survive the day without each other, and the latter one, when she returns, is to show how much we both missed each other.

"How was your day?" she asks me first, this time.
"You stole my line," I complain.
"I want to be the first one to know today because usually, it's always you asking me this."
"Alright, ladies first." I lead her towards the staircase to go to the bedroom. "My day was perfect. I had some important calls to make. I also spoke to Dad and

Mom, and they are going to Edinburg for a week to meet my aunt who stays there."

"Oh," she sighs. "So, you will be busy managing the work in your father's absence next week."
"Kind of. Why? Do we have any other plans?"

We reach the bedroom, and she is already taking off her heels. She doesn't like to wear them much. I know the next thing to come off is her black satin hair tie holding her thick dark ponytail.

"No plans, as I am equally busy next week," she mentions, freeing her long hair as she removes her hair tie and the bobby pins, and I stand behind her mesmerized.
"How was your day?" I finally get to ask, and her excitement is back. Work always excites her and gives her a thrill, nothing else can.

"It was a perfect day. We cracked that Intel deal I was telling you about last week, and soon we are going to begin the project implementation."
"Oh wow, that's a piece of big news, Taani. I knew you would crack that deal. You've spent sleepless nights working on it, and hard work always pays. We need to celebrate."

The Intel deal is only the tip of the iceberg. The bigger deal she is desperately trying to crack is with the RC Group of Companies, the one which even her father couldn't. So, she has made it her mission to fulfill her Dad's dream of acquiring this deal and working day and night for it.
I hug her, and she turns around to give me a peck on the lips.

"Thank you, Sameer. It would not have been possible without you. You also have spent sleepless nights letting me work. So, the credit goes to you too, baby."
"Anything for you," I kiss her back.

After we pull away to breathe again, Taani takes off her jacket and begins to unbutton her shirt mindlessly. She is so engrossed in talking about her day that she doesn't realize how she is turning me on by trying to give a strip show. I can clearly see the lace of her bra peeking from inside, and the hunger in my eyes doesn't go unnoticed by Taani, who turns around quickly, facing the mirror, looking away from me.

I reach behind her, and my fingers slide around her waist, unbuttoning the last two buttons of her shirt. She gasps as I nuzzle my lips over her earlobe while helping her take off her shirt, leaving her only in her lacy bra and trousers.

"Nothing I haven't seen before," I remind Taani before turning her to me again and taking her lips.

We have explored each other's upper bodies to our heart's content, but that's all we do when we make out. The slow kiss turns sensual as Taani guides me to unhook the final piece covering her upper body, and I do so eagerly. The moment I unhook it, planning to take it off, she holds her palms in front of her to not let the fabric fall and smiles devilishly, pulling away from me.

"Thanks for the help. I am famished. Can we continue this post-dinner?"

"Your timing is great," I mock, breathing hard, fully aroused now.

"Please…" she pouts, and all my panting turns into a wide smile for her.

"Dinner and your dinner partner will be waiting for you down. Change and come soon."

"You haven't had your dinner yet? Sameer, I told you not to wait for me. I don't want you to stay hungry."

I softly swat her soft buttocks.

"You keep me hungry all day as it is, baby. Stop being so formal. I like having meals with my wife. Now take a quick shower and come soon."

Pressing a kiss on her forehead again, I make my way out of the room, giving her the privacy to freshen up.

Post-dinner, when we get back to the room, Taani is confused at seeing the room decorated with dim lights, which weren't there until we were here sometime back. I wait for her reaction, and the moment she sees her favourite red velvet cake with *'Happy 1st Month Anniversary'* written on it, she puts her palm over her mouth in surprise and turns to me.

"Seriously? Is it one month already? How could I forget the date? But who celebrates one-month anniversary, Sameer?"

I walk to her lazily with a grin.

"We will. I think it's romantic to celebrate monthly anniversaries."

She sighs in pleasure and looks back at the cake as I wrap my arms around her and rest my chin on her shoulder.

"You liked the surprise?"
"I loved it."

She turns and kisses my cheeks before settling her luscious lips on mine. We kiss like bunnies and finally cut the cake together, wishing each other loads of happiness for the future. Cuddling up on the couch, we talk about how it all felt like a dream from the time we got married and now, even completed one month of it successfully. Soon her eyes start drooping as she's tired and needs to wake up early again. So, just like every other night, I carry her to bed. It's become our routine now, and I love it. We cuddle up, kiss and softly make out by grinding our bodies against each other, my palms fondling and squeezing her soft breasts while she keeps kissing me all over my lips, neck, and chest until we finally doze off.

CHAPTER 12

Taani

TWO MONTHS LATER

It's been three months since my marriage to Sameer, and my world has already changed. There was no one to keep a check on my diet before and make sure I had eaten my meals, but ever since we got married, Sameer has taken over that role. He never lets me skip my breakfast at home, even if I have an early meeting. There have been days when Sameer had fed me breakfast while I was getting ready so that I was not late for work. Actually, it was all because of him that I woke up late one day. Though we slept on time the other night, Sameer's mouth on my breasts woke me up at midnight, and I let him devour me the way he wanted to. Though we didn't make love that night, he touched me down there where I ached the most for him, between my legs, and it felt like I was floating; it was bliss. It started with a gentle touch of his hands, and a few strokes of his fingertips over my silky fabric below, yet it was the most pleasurable sensation I had ever felt, so much so that I didn't want this heavenly feeling to stop. So, the point is, we woke up late, and Sameer had to feed me.

Whenever I return from the meetings and check my phone, I always find his message asking me to have lunch on time. Once, he even cooked my favourite paneer burji and surprised me by getting it to my office. I was just deciding what to order when I saw him, already in my cabin with my favourite dish, waiting to have lunch with me.

These little gestures have stolen my heart, and I am falling in love, bit by bit, with the man I am married to.

"Taani?" Sameer's mother's voice brings my attention back to the phone call.

I speak to her almost every alternate day, if not daily, due to my work routine, and she's the coolest mom-in-law one could get.

"Yes, I can hear you." I chew my bottom lip for being absent-minded, but I can't help it. Sameer and his thoughts have started to grab all my attention, even at work, these days. "You still didn't tell me what should I send for you along with Sameer?" I ask her.

Sameer is flying to London in a week as there are urgent business issues he has to deal with along with his Dad. I can't stop him since he's already sacrificing a lot by staying with me in India. He's only going for a month and then will be back again with me. I am going to miss him. In fact, I have already begun to miss him.

"Oh, how I wish you could also come along with

him to London," aunty sighs. "But I know you are busy."

"I wish I wasn't that busy, Aunty, but this new deal I am trying to acquire is really important."

"I know, sweetheart. Sameer has told us how much this deal means to you. Don't worry. We will wait. You take your time and send my boy home. I am waiting to pamper him."

"Please pamper him. He needs it as here it is the other way around. Sameer is always the one to take care of me and pamper me instead."

Aunty laughs at my remark, but I know she is proud of what Sameer is doing.

"Isn't he the perfect husband for you?" she teases.

"That he is," I agree, and we continue the discussion.

When I finish the call, I check my phone and delete the unwanted notifications. One such notification I see is from the BookMyShow app, notifying me of a new Marvel movie that was released today. I know how much Sameer loves Marvel movies, and he always makes it a point to watch these at his London home's private theatre again and again. I am sure he knows about this movie and must be eager to watch it. That's when I realize what I can do to return the favour that Sameer keeps showering on me.

Sameer is busy working on his laptop in the bedroom when I surprise him by coming home early.

"Hello, busy boy." I ruffle his sexy hair, slide my arms around his neck from behind and give him a kiss on the cheek.

"Taani?" He sounds surprised, as though he cannot believe his eyes. "What are you doing home early? Are you feeling sick?"

Pushing his laptop away, Sameer pulls me on his lap. I give his face a thorough once-over. He's trimmed his French beard today, and I love how distinguished it makes him look.

"I am fine. In fact, absolutely fine, now that I am on your lap."

He swallows whatever else he is about to ask as I kiss his full lips. After sucking his lips like he does mine, I finally pull away.

"Get dressed. We are going out."

"Out?" He looks a bit disoriented.

"Yes, to watch your favourite movie. It's released today."

He blinks once, twice, thrice, and then his jaw hangs open.

"But you had a conference this evening. What about that?"

"I postponed it to tomorrow afternoon."

I start unbuttoning his shirt, and he lets me. The feel of his toned abs against my fingers makes my body shudder with yearning, but we can't indulge in making out as we don't have much time left for the movie to begin.

"You postponed it just for a movie?" He asks as I slide down the shirt from his shoulders and give him feathery kisses at the nape of his neck.

"I postponed it to watch the movie with my husband. The man who has given me everything without even me asking."

He is about to argue, but I shut him up with a scorching kiss, and he gives in. Just like a moth is drawn to a flame, he grinds our bodies, and I can feel the heat emanating from his rigid length to just where I need it. Many thoughts run through my head regarding tonight. I want to give Sameer his share of the happiness that he deserves from me. Before I can act on those ideas, Sameer breaks the kiss and cups my face, licking his lips, which have my gloss all over them. He loves my lip gloss, and has told me that many times.

"What time is the show?" he asks.

I check my watch.
"06:45 pm. It means we have only an hour to get ready and reach the multiplex. And I know you don't want to miss the beginning."

"Damn, no!!"

He helps me get down from his lap, and whilst I head to the washroom to freshen up, Sameer changes into jeans and a T-shirt, and we drive to the nearest multiplex to begin our movie date.

****

I never knew Sameer was a kid at heart and that watching this movie would bring such joy to his face. I have no idea about this movie or even the series, but Sameer keeps introducing me to the characters as and when they appear and updating me on the storyline. Sci-fi thrillers or fantasies are not the types of movies I usually watch. I like old classical Bollywood movies that Dad and I used to watch together. Yet here I am, thoroughly enjoying this two-hour show with Sameer, sitting next to him and cuddling up his arm, entwining our fingers and kissing his hand in between, while watching the movie. Sameer keeps glancing at me from time to time as though a bit confused by my sudden 'touchy gestures', but God knows, today, I cannot keep my hands off him.

Just then, a scene appears on the screen where the hero is kissing his woman, and Sameer's gaze returns to mine as my nails dig into his hard biceps. He leans closer, and I know what he needs. Sliding my fingers at his nape, I pull him for a scorching kiss in the darkness of the movie hall. Thankfully, we have VIP couple seats, and there's no one beside us. Sitting at the corner seat and kissing in a multiplex was one of the naughty desires on my wish list when I was in college, and tonight even that came to life, all thanks to the man I was falling hard for.

After the movie, I surprise Sameer again by reserving a table at his favourite restaurant, where we have his choice of dinner. He is overwhelmed by my attention and the way I am in no rush to head home and start working. It's strange. I don't want this time between us to end. I want to stick by his side, be around him, do what he likes, give him what he wants and most importantly, pamper him with everything I can tonight. It's a beautiful feeling to see Sameer so happy. I can do anything to keep that smile intact on his face forever.

We finish eating and reach the car to head back home when Sameer grabs me by my waist and pins me to the car door before I can get inside.

"This is one of the best days of my life, Taani. I want you to know that." Sameer's husky voice, laced with tender emotion, proves how happy he is that we spent the entire evening with each other.

"I know," I reply, palming his cheek. "It's one of my best days too."

We keep gazing into each other's eyes.
"I'll miss you, Sameer. I wish I could come with you to London, but-"
"I'll come back sooner than you realize."
"Hmm."

And my eyes tear up. But thankfully, a car honking breaks our eye lock and I get the time to wipe my eyes before getting inside the car. Sameer drives us home unaware of my present yearning for him.

Sameer

I've never been this pampered by Taani before. She came home early from work to take me out on a movie date, then planned a dinner at my favourite restaurant and now, after coming home, instead of turning on her laptop and working, she is on the bed, letting me love her. I want the same too because tonight she looks sexy, wearing satin babydoll lingerie, and I hope she's wearing this to seduce me. I think Taani is a bit upset that I am heading to London after a week and won't be here for a month. I wouldn't have gone if it wasn't so urgent. My heart desired to either stay back or take Taani along, but none of that was possible at the moment. Taani is working on cracking her dream project at the moment with the RC Group of companies, something that was her Dad's wish till the very end of his life. As Taani has taken over all her father's wishes and is racing to accomplish them, this deal means everything to her. She had also taken a few ideas from me on what best she could do to ensure they agreed to do business with her company. I am fully confident that she would soon get a call from that company and that deal would be signed. Even God wouldn't be able to neglect my Taani's hard work.

Leaving all these thoughts aside at the moment, I continue to devour my wife, who is more than willing to let me do the same. I kiss a trail down her skin, from her neck to her little belly button, and just like every other time, I restrain myself from going further down. That's the line she has drawn between us so far, and I would never cross it until she wants me to. When I am about to kiss her back upwards, Taani grips my shoulder, pausing me. I raise my chin to meet her sparkling eyes, unleashing a dark lust I never saw in them before.

I look at her, waiting impatiently to know what she is thinking. My heart tells me Taani wants me to go ahead. I can read it all over her face, yet I don't want to assume anything, lest I am wrong.

I can see the urgency in her eyes to continue; and sense the hesitation in her mind.

"I need words, Taani," I demand.

She chews her lower lip and whispers something. My Taani has always been clear about what she wants and is bold enough to convey it. So, this time, I urge her to clear my doubt and her intention—so we don't misread each other.

"What is it that you want, Taani?" I ask her again, my grip on her hips tightening.

Her pulse picks up underneath me as she tries to frame the exact words I need to hear from her.

"Make me yours tonight, Sameer. In every way you can," she purrs.

As soon as she utters those words that I have been longing to hear, heat passes through my entire body, and I can feel the tightening in my boxers at the thought of claiming Taani as my wife. I still can't believe what she said. Did she really say it, or am I hallucinating? Not thinking further, I slide up to meet Taani's face. She gasps in surprise when my fingers stroke her soft cheeks instead of getting directly into the act.

"You sure about this?" I ask. "I don't want you to take this decision only to make me happy or in the heat of the moment, Taani. This is a huge step for both of us. And besides, you know this will make the one-month separation harder for both of us. We will crave for it, for each other, and I don't want you to lose your focus from your impending deal. So, think wisely before giving me this permission tonight."

Taani takes a moment to comprehend.

"This..." she smiles, kissing my palm. "The sensitivity you show towards every decision, desire and focus of my life is what has stolen my heart, Sameer. What I am asking from you tonight is your right. It's been your right ever since you married me. It's the least I can offer you for all you have done for me as a partner. I don't want to deprive us of this need anymore. Give me everything you got because it's mine. And take everything I have in me because it's yours. We are one, Sameer. Make me feel like we are one."

I grin at her reply. My fingers automatically reach for that last piece of lace covering her body from my eyes.

"You and I, and I and you have already been one since the day we took our first breath, baby. Tonight is just a formality."

I reward her with a kiss while my fingers slide her fabric aside and dip inside her wetness, touching the inner folds of her bare skin. Everything else is a blur as we moan in unison. Taani is goddamn perfection. She's the kind of woman I had always desired and craved. Only she could satiate this unquenched thirst in me, and it begins from this very moment. No woman ever has nor will bring out these carnal desires in me except her. It will always be her. My Taani. My wife. The love of my life.

I devour her sensitive skin, which was forbidden to me, with my fingers and mouth. Her breathing quickens as my fingertips trail in and out of her sensitive flesh while my lips plant kisses all over her body. A yearning so intense takes hold of my body as her hands slide from my toned biceps to my bare back, pulling me closer. She bucks her hip as I continue with my sweet torture and gives a loud moan, basking in the pleasure I am showering upon her. I look up at her. She looks beautiful in the throes of passion, her skin glistening with a golden hue and cheeks flushed tomato red. Taani pulls my face to kiss me in order to subside the burning ache in her body. I want to hold her, pleasure her and claim her all at once. It's a heady feeling none of us can ignore any longer. We have been waiting for this moment when we can finally be one. We have teased each other enough. It's time for me to give her the greatest pleasure she has ever experienced and to complete our relationship. As soon as she is ready to take me in, I press a kiss on her lips again.

"This might hurt you initially, Taani, but I promise it will get better," I keep planting kisses on her face. "I will try to be as gentle as possible. Feel free to stop me anytime you are uncomfortable. I won't mind at all. For me, your comfort comes before anything else."

She stops me from kissing her and looks intently at me as if she is madly in love with me, especially after this show of support I gave her that I was ready to stop at once if she didn't want to go ahead.

Taani softly kisses my chin.
"You talk too much, Sameer. Just get to work, or let me do it."

I am tongue-tied when Taani slides her hand down slowly, grazing over my boxers before slipping her hand inside as though she wants to have her fill of me. I liked her touching me and feeling up my body every time we made out, but never in my mind did I think she would be bold enough to touch me down there on her own. Her touch is soft at first, unsure in its actions, but then she finds her rhythm and starts pleasuring me. Taani's actions are unstoppable, and I bite back a groan as I have no control over my body now.

"That's enough," I grin. "Remember, you asked for it," I say hoarsely before shredding the remaining piece of clothes from our bodies as the need to unite consumes us. Uniting our bodies in one swift move and breaking the barrier between us, I immediately fuse our mouths to prevent Taani from screaming in pain.

Once she composes herself, I rock us together to the world of ecstasy. Watching her eyes dilate as our bodies unite, her soft whimpers, which I soothe with a kiss, her soft pants and the movement of her body in rhythm with mine, is something I will cherish my whole life, and I know this won't be the only time I see these expressions of hers. I feel extremely lucky and blessed to have my wife the way I wanted to, forever, till eternity. And the night has only begun...

CHAPTER 13

Taani

I think all my alarms rang, and none of them could wake us up on time; we were that spent. Last night was the best night of my life where I gave Sameer that right on me that I'd deprived him of till now. One thing I learned from my marriage to Sameer was that marriage is not a business deal where we can manipulate the risks and weigh the pros and cons at every step we take as life partners. It's a journey of two people learning their way around each other and creating space in each other's hearts; it's a give-and-take relationship, and Sameer has clearly marked his territory in every corner of my heart with his sweet and caring persona.

With all these thoughts running in my head, I head to take a shower when Sameer joins me inside the shower cubicle. I didn't want to wake him up early so I let him sleep for some more time until I cooked breakfast for him. But it seemed like the sound of my shower woke him up, or maybe it was the empty, cold bed where I'd left him alone. Last night, letting him take control over my body, where he had seen, touched and felt all of me, was easy, but today, in broad daylight, when he eyes me hungrily, I want to hide myself, but I don't. Without a word, I allow him to take over my body again, and the shower, which would have lasted for a few minutes, carries on for an hour; where we spend time soaping and cleaning each other until we have no energy left in us, and hit the bed again.

For two days, we have had the same routine. We wake up late in the afternoon, have lunch, check our work emails, which is the only time we don't see each other, and try to finish our work in a few hours. We have early dinner and hit the bed again, making love throughout the night until sunrise. I never knew I had a wild streak in me and so much stamina to carry on making love with my husband for hours, but I am enjoying every bit of it.

Three more days and Sameer will fly to London, and I want us to spend maximum time with each other before that. I have been working from home for the past three days and have told my assistant Pooja to contact me via phone in case of emergencies. Today, I am helping Sameer pack his bags, and we are talking about his flight schedule when I suddenly feel giddy and fall unconscious.

****

I stir and open my eyes to see Sameer talking to my family doctor, Sheetal. My sister, Vidhi, is also here. Why is she here? Who called her? I try to sit on the bed, catching their attention. Sameer is the first one to reach me and help me sit.

"How are you feeling now?" he asks, resting the pillow behind my back as I sit.

"I am fine. What happened to me?"

"Physical exertion, work stress, lack of energy, call it whatever you like," Vidhi mutters, sitting on the other side of the bed, holding my hand, and teasing Sameer. "Sameer, what did you do to make my sister drain all her energy?"

Sameer reddens, but he replies cheekily to my sister's teasing.

"The same things that Vansh does to drain yours."

Vidhi's mouth hangs open, and though she tries her best to hide her blush, she fails. But then she looks at my face, and her eyes widen in surprise. I know what that look is for. Vidhi is the only one who knew despite being married to Sameer, we both had not consummated our marriage, and now she just discovered that we did.

Sheetal walks up to Sameer and passes him the prescription.

"Sameer, give this medicine to Taani. She'll be fine in 2 -3 days. She needs ample rest to regain her health. There's nothing to worry about."

"Sure, Doctor."

Asking me to take care, Doctor Sheetal leaves, and I am left alone with Vidhi as Sameer also heads out to ask one of the servants to bring the prescribed medicines.

"So? It happened finally," Vidhi teases, nudging my arm.

"Hmm. And stop right there. We are not discussing that."

She giggles on seeing my hesitation, but that's how I am. I cannot discuss my sex life with my sister. No way!!

"But don't you think you need to slow down a bit. I mean, at this rate, he will make you faint daily." She teases me again.

"Shut up. And no, Sameer has nothing to do with me fainting. I am just stressing about work as usual. You know I am waiting for the RC group of companies to schedule this meeting with us so that I can convince them how good our deal is, but since they are delaying, I am getting jittery. Moreover, Sameer is leaving for London in two days, and I am already missing him."

Vidhi's smile fades as she becomes serious.

"So much work stress is not good for you, Taani. And poor Sameer, he just cancelled his flight."

"What??" I snap.

"Yea, he did that when the doctor was here. Obviously, he can't leave you when you are sick."

Sameer returns to the room, and poor guy, he is probably blaming himself for exerting me and feels guilty about my ill health.

"Sameer, you can't cancel your trip," I declare as he reaches the bed.

"We will talk about that later. Right now, drink this. It will hydrate you."

He gives me coconut water, which I drink despite not feeling like it, as both Vidhi and Sameer insist on it. Vidhi stays back for some time since Vansh is out of the city. Vansh had called me and conveyed his wishes to get well soon. I am really fortunate to have wonderful friends and family. Once Vidhi leaves, I tell Sameer not to cancel his trip to London and not to inform his parents about this incident. I don't want them to be worried. But though he agrees not to tell his parents, Sameer is unwilling to fly for work, and for now, I accept his decision.

That night Sameer checks with me if I want him to sleep in the other room so that I can relax alone on the bed, without him, but I don't let him sleep anywhere else. At present, I need him the most; his presence calms me. He is my husband, and I want him on my bed every night. So, before he can argue, I pull him onto the bed and cuddle against him. Sameer gives in, and we spend the night in each other's arms, getting our share of sleep.

Sameer

I check Taani's temperature to ensure she has no fever while she is in deep slumber, snoring softly on the bed. It's quite early to wake her up as it's hardly 07:30 am, and she needs rest as per the doctor's suggestion. I still don't understand how Taani fell sick so suddenly. Did I really exert her this much? She has her mind occupied with so much work stress, and I exerted her physically too. No wonder her body couldn't take it. I stare at my gorgeous wife's sleeping form, before walking out of the room to make some coffee for myself. Taani needs rest, and I am going to ensure she gets it. I have even taken her phone along with me so that she doesn't get disturbed by her work calls or notifications.

Just when I am finishing my coffee and reading the morning local newspaper, Taani's phone rings. I am in the living room, and my wife is still sleeping, so I answer the call on her behalf. It's her assistant Pooja.

"Hi, Pooja,"

Pooja is surprised to hear my voice on Taani's phone and requests me to let her speak to Taani.

"She is resting, Pooja. I can't wake her up. If you have any messages, tell me and I will let her know."

"Ma'am has some sudden meetings lined up for today. If she can make it to the office by evening, she will be able to attend that."

"Today evening?" I reconfirm.

"Yes, Sir."

"It's not possible this evening, Pooja. She is sick and needs rest. Whatever meeting has suddenly come up; can you please reschedule them after 2-3 days? By then, Taani will be in better health to come to work."

"But Sir, I can't reschedule them until I speak to Ma'am."

"I am your Ma'am's husband, Pooja, and I am sure you and I both want her to be healthy above everything else."

"Of course, Sir." I sense some hesitation in Pooja's voice, but she finally gets my point and agrees to postpone the meeting. I disconnect the call and continue flipping the pages of the newspaper. I am going to make a healthy breakfast for Taani. After that, I have to call Dad and inform him about my delay in travelling to London. I know it will incur some losses for my company if I don't arrive there on time, but I can risk anything to be with my wife when she is feeling sick and needs me the most around her.

****

Post lunch, after ensuring Taani took her medicines and rested, I was working on my laptop when the door to the study room opened, and Taani barged inside. She looks miffed.

"You spoke to my assistant today?" she asks, keeping her tone in check, but I can still sense something is amiss. She is not happy.

"Yeah, she had called this morning while you were sleeping."

"And you didn't tell me?"

"You just heard me, Taani." I get up from the chair to reach her. "You were sleeping, which was more important than attending that call. That's why I didn't tell you and asked her to leave a message with me."

"You didn't ask her to just leave a message, Sameer. You took an important decision on my behalf."

What? I am dumbstruck but soon realize what she means.

"Yes, I did. I asked Pooja to reschedule that meeting which had suddenly popped up, and moreover, they were never on your agenda anyway. So what?"

"So what?"

She threw the phone angrily on the couch, and luckily it did not break. I have never seen her this angry. I think Pooja called her again to inform her about the meeting. While looking after her health and continuing my work, I really forgot to tell Taani about Pooja's morning call.

"Taani, what happened?"

"What happened?" she repeats, closing the distance between us. "I missed the only chance I had to meet the CEO of RC Group of Companies today, only because *you* asked Pooja to reschedule it, Sameer."

What? RC Group of companies? How was I supposed to know the meeting request was from them? I never asked, and nor did Pooja inform me. I can understand Taani's anger now. She was slogging hard for this one meeting with that company, and Taani missed it because of me.

"Taani, I didn't know it was their meeting." I try to grip her arms, but she shoves them away.

"How could you do this, Sameer? You know I want that deal so bad. It's not just about the deal or the company; it was one of my dad's wishes that Gupta Industries collaborate for a project or two with the RC Group. And now, one wrong decision from you, and I lost that chance."

Gosh!! I rake my fingers through my hair in frustration. I can't believe this happened.

"Taani, we can speak to them again, and it's not that this was your last chance. Ask Pooja to contact them again for the next best date to meet. I'm sure they will understand you were not well and hence couldn't meet them today, and...."

"Don't." She interrupts me. "I don't need your advice anymore, not after you made such a huge blunder."

"Taani, c'mon, I really didn't know. I didn't do it on purpose. You know that."

"Yes. I do, Sameer. I know you didn't do any of this on purpose, but it has snatched away what I needed the most. Just one opportunity is what I wanted, and I lost it because of you. Damn!!"

She turns away in anger. I can't see her like this.

"Let's call Pooja and ask her to schedule it again."

I take her phone from the couch where she had thrown it, but Taani's voice interrupts me.
"You think I didn't try doing that?" she asks. "Their CEO is flying to the USA tomorrow and might not return for a few months."

I am still thinking of ways to salvage this situation, but Taani continues.
"I gave you the right to my heart, body and soul, Sameer. I did not give you the right to make decisions on my behalf and interfere in my business."
My heart skips a beat. Did I hear her correctly? Before I can ask her why she said that, Taani turns to me. I keep my patience in check, considering she is still weak.

"Taani, calm down. You are stressing your body again."
"*You* are stressing me, Sameer. *You*. If it weren't for your stupid decision, we wouldn't even be having this conversation. You turned away the best opportunity of my life."
"I did it because of your health. You are still weak. How would you have managed that meeting even if I hadn't asked to reschedule it?"

"That was my lookout. I would have dealt with it," Taani scowls. "Even before marriage and your presence in my life, I have been sick and have managed my work efficiently. And it never happened that an opportunity knocked at my door and left, just because I was sleeping and my husband made the decision for me."

Anger bubbles inside me, but all I do right now is clench my jaw and let her vent out her feelings. She is already in tears by the time she reaches me and looks at me.

"This is exactly why I didn't want to marry. It takes away the control from you."

"Mind your words, Taani. You are degrading our marriage now. And this has nothing to do with what happened today. I thought I had that much right over you that I could think about your wellness and make decisions accordingly. You don't have to get our marriage in between all this. But you are talking as if that deal meant everything to you, more so than our marriage."

"Yes, it did. This deal and everything related to my business has always been above our marriage, and you know that already, Sameer. I had already conveyed this to you, and you signed up for this marriage aware of that." She screams in frustration.

I am shocked. Yes, I know what her father's company means to her, but I never thought coming to this point in our relationship, Taani would still keep it above me and our marriage.

She squeezes her eyes shut and, opening them again, glares at me.

"I shouldn't have made this mistake." She mutters, meaning every word she says.

I am losing my mind now.

"How can you say something like that about our marriage? You are talking as if someone forced you to marry me, and you don't give a damn about it now." I ask again, only to hear her shout back.

"Yes, I don't give a damn about our marriage if this is what it gives me in return. Failure!!" she snaps.

I stare at her in silence. She doesn't mean it, does she?

Taani shakes her head in disappointment. "Vansh's Daadi coaxed me to think of your proposal, and it clouded my mind. My age, the need to have a life partner and Daadi's advice on not losing this chance are the factors that made me marry you. I wish I knew I was making the biggest mistake of my life, Sameer," she adds, and that's it. I lost every ounce of my control this time.

"Yes." I snap. "You are right. You made a big mistake marrying me, Taani. I thought you married me out of your choice. But it seems I was wrong. So yes, you have every right to regret this decision. I am sorry you had to go through all this because of me. I am really very sorry."

Though I apologized, my tone betrayed me. I was hurt, angry and disappointed at Taani's declaration. I turn around towards the door and leave her alone. Probably it's for the best that she stays alone and ponders over what just happened and if she still held true to what she just said, then maybe staying alone is what Taani Gupta really wants in her life. I was a fool to think she would welcome my love and support in her life. She doesn't need me. She never did, and she never will.

CHAPTER 14

Taani

I couldn't sleep a wink last night as I was working on salvaging the situation Sameer was partly responsible for. He knew how much my work meant to me, yet he failed to convey a simple but important message from my assistant. He should have let me decide what was necessary for my company. But all my efforts were in vain. I couldn't get an appointment with the CEO of the RC Group as he was travelling. And there was no guarantee I would get one anytime soon, considering they are already renowned and at the top of their game to allow a mid-size company like mine to present my business proposal. I had unknowingly missed the only window I had to fulfill Dad's wish of collaborating with them.

I didn't realize when I slept on my desk last night, but, as usual, today morning, when I woke up, I found myself on the bed. That could only mean Sameer carried me, like every other night. The only difference this time was that he didn't sleep beside me. The other side of my bed is cold and unused. Suddenly the flashback of everything I told Sameer last night, in anger, comes back to haunt me. I vented all my anger and disappointment on him for missing this opportunity. And wait!! Now that I remember, I even said what I shouldn't have. How could I regret our marriage or having him in my life? Gosh!! I put my palm over my mouth. Why the hell did I say that? My mind goes back to last night and the expressions on his face when we had this argument. It had hurt and devastation written all over it. He had tried his best to convince me that he didn't do it on purpose. But last night, I was on a roll. I wasn't in a sane mind; I didn't even give him a chance to explain. I kept hurling accusations at him, hurting him in the process, and now that I realize my mistake, I don't know how I will face him. I can't even imagine how shattered he must have felt, with me making a mockery of our marriage. I get down from the bed and go to look for Sameer.

I look for him in the guest room where I thought Sameer would have slept last night, but he is not there, nor does the bed look slept on. Where can he go? I look for him frantically in the entire villa, but he is nowhere to be seen. I rush back to our bedroom, and that's when I notice his missing luggage. The bag I had packed for his London trip a few days ago was missing. Damn! He left? He left for London? Without even letting me know? How could he do that? My phone!! Where is my phone? I look for it and find it on the bedside table. I quickly grab it to call him when I see his WhatsApp message from two hours ago.

'I am boarding my flight to London in the next few minutes, Taani. I didn't want to leave your side, especially after knowing you held me responsible for your lost business opportunity. I wanted to stay back and help clear your misconception. But you are right. With me beside you, you are losing your control over your work. I am distracting you. I don't want all your efforts and hard work so far to go in vain. I want to see you succeed, reach new heights and bag every deal, every project you ever dreamed of. You deserve it all. I am sorry for deciding to reschedule your meeting. Had I known it was from the RC Group, I would never have made that mistake. It wasn't intentional. You were sick, and I wanted you to heal before taking over the company responsibilities again. I am sorry because I know how much that hurt you, but I don't regret it as your health always comes first, and everything else is secondary. If you were in my position and I was sick, wouldn't you keep my health above the rest? Think about it. Still, my love and concern for you turned toxic for your business, and I regret that deeply. I wish there was a way I could rectify this and bring you back what you lost, but I can't.*

I am deeply sorry for the mess, Taani, and I wish you all the best for your future endeavors. I am just giving you the space you need to fix things and think about what you said last night. Staying there would have made me guiltier, especially to face a woman who thinks our marriage is the biggest mistake of her life. I hope you said that in the heat of the moment and didn't mean it. I thought we had something special between us, and my love was your strength. But that same love turned out to be your weakness, and I can never see you weak. I am just a phone call away,

Taani. I am still your husband. I am still the man who loves you unconditionally, and you still mean the world to me. You are my whole world, and I hope to be a part of your little world again, but only if you want me to. Until then, please take care of your health. Don't forget to have your medicines on time; Completing your medication course is important. Don't skip your breakfast. I have told the chef and your assistant, Pooja, to keep reminding you of the same. And most importantly, don't stress over your work. Eventually, we always get what we deserve in our lives, and I am confident the RC Group of companies will contact you again soon and agree to your business proposal because you are the best.

Take care and stay happy.

The moment I read his message, tears streamed down my face. Sameer left me all alone? When I needed his support, he left me. Yes, I know I hurt him last night with my words, but even I was hurt and angry with everything that happened. And above all, he is aware of my moods, my anger and my intrinsic need to have control over my business more than anyone else in my life. Still, he left me alone to deal with the repercussions. It's my fault. Yes, maybe it is. But he shouldn't have left without informing me. And if he thinks I will call him and ask him to come back, he is wrong. I am obviously remorseful for telling him I regret our marriage, but he should have been here for me to apologize. Instead, he chose to flee from the situation and is putting all this on me that I want space to work and fix my issues. So be it, Sameer Khanna. I have lived alone for almost half of my life and still can. If that's what you want me to do again,

I'll prove to you that I can live alone. But, I know it's easier said than done.

It's been three weeks since Sameer was gone, and I feel heartbroken. I resume my office again, and my chef ensures I never leave home without having breakfast, which is always hot and ready, just like how Sameer had advised them. Even though I don't feel hungry sometimes, I dare not skip it, knowing it might hurt Sameer. At the office, Pooja is constantly chasing me during lunchtime and ordering healthy meals for me, and again, I know it's because Sameer has asked her to do so. Despite staying oceans away, he is still looking after me, and only someone who loves you unconditionally will do that. I am so blessed to be loved by someone like him, and what I gave him in return; was only misery and pain. I know how deeply hurt he is. I have to apologize to him, leaving aside my ego and the regret of losing a potential client like the RC Group. Sameer is right in saying we only get things we truly deserve. Maybe the stars were not aligned for me to do business with them currently. I'm sure I will get another opportunity soon, and I'll make sure not to lose it.

The most important thing for me to do at this point is to win Sameer's love and trust back. I have to let him know that our relationship means something to me too, and it's not that I don't respect it. I feel extremely guilty whenever I remember how rudely I snapped at Sameer, stating I made a mistake in marrying him. It's not easy for any husband to listen to those cruel words from his wife. And it is Sameer's goodness that he didn't utter a word about our fight to his parents. I am still in touch with them, and his mother always tells me how much they miss me, especially Sameer, who has totally immersed himself in his work so that he doesn't miss me. I know why he is doing this. He wants to keep himself occupied so that the pain I unintentionally gave him doesn't engulf him more.

The same is my condition here. It doesn't matter how busy I am during the entire day, but when I am back home, I miss Sameer's essence around me. I miss his presence, his hugs and his kisses when I return from work. Nowadays, I don't even sleep on my bed anymore as it holds too many memories. Without him, the bed is cold and uninviting. I miss Sameer's touch. I sleep on the couch instead, and on most days, I end up sleeping at my work table for the whole night because Sameer is not here to carry me back to bed. I miss my husband and my friend; one I loved coming back home to. I miss the intimacy we shared. I ache for his touch and yearn for his presence around me to see me, take care of my little things and give me the warmth and cuddle that I could get from one man only, and that is—my husband. I miss my Sameer. I miss him like hell.

The door knocks, and Vidhi enters my cabin, holding a box which looks like a cake.
"Can I come in, Boss?" Vidhi teases.
"Come inside, Vidhi."
I try to compose myself and fake a smile, as that is what I now do when I meet people. This never happened when I was with Sameer. I genuinely was happy and looked contended, but now that he is gone, I feel hollow once again. It's my mistake, I know. These three weeks were enough to kill my ego and put some sense in my head that my heart was

correct and I needed to mend my relationship with Sameer on priority. I miss him a lot.

"What is that?" I ask as Vidhi puts the box on my table before me.

"Don't tell me you forgot."

"Forgot what?" I shrug.

"Your fourth month marriage anniversary, Taani."

My mouth hangs open. Oh yes, it's been four months since my marriage to Sameer today. In my misery, I didn't even wish him and neither did he. We celebrated our anniversary with a cake and simple gifts every month, so why didn't he do anything for me this time?

"You know, I always thought Vansh is very romantic," Vidhi continues to open the box while talking to me. "But your Sameer has overtaken him!! He is in London busy with his work, yet he booked this cake specially for you from your favourite place, along with yellow tulips, which you love, and your favourite chocolates. Can any husband be so adorable?" she blinks cutely, looking at me.

I am stunned. Despite being angry, Sameer didn't forget today's date and also kept the tradition of giving me cake, flowers and chocolates intact.

"And hold on. I have something else for you, which he wanted me to give you today. One second."

She picks up my intercom receiver and asks Pooja to get something from the reception. I am confused. What else are we waiting for? Pooja comes in with another huge box.

"And now, what is this?" I inquire.

Pooja keeps it on the table and leaves.

"This is your gift. Sameer gave it to me before flying to London." Vidhi replies, passing me the golden gift-wrapped box. It's big. Like a photo frame or something. What is it? Vidhi, just like the rest of the Kapoor family, thinks Sameer has gone to London to handle the work there. They have no idea about our little fight and that we are no longer on talking terms. I wanted to message Sameer almost every single day, but I couldn't. I didn't know what to say to him and how?

"I didn't know he met you before flying to London," I mutter, staring at Vidhi, who batted her eyelashes again.

"That was supposed to be a secret until today. He came to the VK Mansion early morning the day he was to leave for London to give me this. He had this gift ready for you and wanted to give it on your fourth-month anniversary. But since he had to leave for London and couldn't give you personally, he asked me to do the honours. So, Mrs. Taani Sameer Khanna, I leave you here with the cake and all your gifts because I have a client call in half an hour. You video call your husband and cut the cake with him. And don't forget to tell me what this gift is, once you open it. Bye, sis. And once again, happy four-month marriage anniversary. Both you and Sameer rock as a couple."

She gives me a tight hug and leaves the cabin. I stare at everything Sameer has sent for me now laid on the table. This man!! He can't stop loving me even if I hurt him badly, and I never want him to stop. I am already on the verge of tears as I open the gift. It's a photo frame, and the moment I turn it around to see it, my heart skips a beat. It's our marriage reception photo with Sameer and me occupying the centre stage. Sameer's parents are at his side, and my father is standing right next to me. Oh, God!! How did he do this? Photoshop? Yes. He must have photoshopped this picture from professionals to add my father's old pic next to me on our wedding family portrait to make it look complete. I remember showing Sameer the old albums two months ago, and he loved this picture of my father in a grey suit, posing solo for a business interview. He got that same pic photoshopped on our wedding picture and had it framed. Now it really looked like Dad was present during our wedding to give his blessings to Sameer and me.

Tears roll down my cheeks, and I find it difficult to breathe. I am ashamed of myself for pushing away the man who has always kept me as his priority. Only Sameer could think of a gift so beautiful and heartwarming for me. Only him!! And I hurt him. I hurt him so badly that now I can literally feel his pain seeping through the walls of my heart.

I really have made a huge mistake by letting Sameer go away and doing nothing about it so far. Not anymore. I am going to rectify my wrongdoings right away, and I don't care about the consequences. I am ready to face every resistance Sameer might show me while I woo him. I am going to make him mine again. I am going to make him believe he is the one I want above everything and everyone else. I am going to move heaven and earth to make him believe in my love, and it begins from now. I wipe my tears and pick the receiver to inform my assistant, Pooja, about my next plan of action.

****
<u>London – One Week Later</u>

I ring the doorbell thrice, and no one answers it yet? How's
that possible? Is anyone at home, or am I at the wrong address? No, it can't be. I definitely know where my husband stays in London, and I can't be wrong about this. It took me a week to wind up everything before flying to London, and the ten-hour direct flight from Delhi to London has exhausted me in ways I cannot even imagine. I need sleep and rest, but not until I open up to someone about this issue first. The pain I gave to Sameer is already killing me, and I need to vent it out for some moral support and advice.

I press the doorbell again, and finally, the door opens. It's my mother-in-law.

"Taani?" She looks surprised, happy and confused, all at once, which is understandable because I didn't inform them of my impromptu visit.

I drop my handbags the moment she opens the door for me.

"I made a mistake," I vent it out. "A huge one. Please help me," I stutter with fresh tears in my eyes.

She stares nervously at me before pulling me in for a hug.

"Oh dear, what happened?"
I hugged her back as tight as I could. She is Sameer's mom, and opening up to her is the best

solution since she can guide me on what to do next. She takes me inside their beautiful mansion and makes me sit on the plush couch before passing me some water to drink. She sits beside me as I drink the water while she strokes my head lovingly. I keep the glass back on the table and hold her hand, telling her everything that happened between me and Sameer that night. She hears me out without interrupting or passing any judgement. I even told her how I felt the very next morning when I came to know Sameer had left for London, about the message he sent on my phone and about the void I felt in the last month in his absence. I tell her everything, and it's only after I unburden myself that I feel a bit better. It might be because I know I am closer to Sameer since I am in London now and also because I have shed a truckload of tears while confessing about this incident to his mother.

Aunty wipes my tears and then palms my face.

"Taani, sweetheart, stop crying. It's okay."
"It's not okay. I hurt him. I can't believe I did that. Sameer loves me so much, and he has proved it at every point, whether we were together or not, and look at what I did? How could I be so selfish? How could I not keep him at the top of my priorities? He doesn't deserve this. He doesn't deserve me...."

Aunty cups my face.
"Taani, mistakes happen, sweetheart, but the best part is they come with learning. We are humans, and every marriage has its own ups and downs. Now coming to what happened between you and Sameer, I can now understand why Sameer didn't look as happy as before after he came here. I sensed

something odd in his behaviour, especially his forced smiles and the way he spent most of the time at work as though purposely avoiding any personal conversations with me and his father. If he had talked to us, it would have made him feel lighter, but anyways, now that you are back, things will work themselves out. He will be happy to see you here just as I am."

I don't know what to say. His mother is putting my mistakes behind me, and I hope Sameer does the same.

"Let's surprise him," Aunty says with renewed excitement. "I won't tell him you are here. Let him come home and get his surprise. Sameer and his father should be back in an hour. I'll take you to your bedroom where you can arrange your stuff and freshen up. We can have dinner together."

"I want to make Sameer's favourite dessert for tonight."

"Now?" She looks surprised.

"Yes, if you don't mind, can I use your kitchen? I'll need only 30 minutes to cook."

"Taani," Aunty chuckles. "Sameer, this kitchen, in fact, this entire house is yours. Do whatever you want and however, you want. You don't need our permission for that. Come, let me show you the house."

I get up with her, but the next moment, I give her another tight hug for all the support she has shown so far.

"Thanks, Mom."

She holds me to herself with more warmth and love.

"You called me Mom and not Aunty. That's a huge change, Taani," she expresses, and my smile returns.

Yes. I just called her Mom, and it was totally unplanned. When we pull away from the hug, she has tears in her eyes.

"That shows how dedicated you are to taking our family as your own and becoming a part of us. I am so happy."

"I am also happy," I nod. "Mom," I use that title again, feeling completely overwhelmed by the term.

I always longed to call someone 'Mom', and now that I have Sameer's mother as mine, I can't wait to develop this bond further.

CHAPTER 15

Sameer

It's been a month since I returned to London, and Taani hasn't messaged me back even once. I can't believe this. Has she really given up on me and our marriage? Did she really mean those words she said that night during our argument? Doesn't she want me back in her life? Or is she angry with me because I left for London without informing her? I have so much going on in my mind from the time all this happened, but I couldn't share it with anyone, let alone with my parents. I can't burden them with Taani and my problems. I've heard Mom and Dad speak to Taani on video calls often, which meant she wasn't breaking off entirely with the family. Does she want me to message her first? I would have. I really want to, but what if Taani doesn't want the same? I had left her a message just before boarding my flight and had clearly mentioned that I was a phone call away if she wanted me back. But she never messaged or called. What does that mean?

Taani might have forgotten her role as my wife, but I haven't ignored that even for a second. Like a good husband, I have been in touch with her assistant Pooja and Taani's Chef at Gupta Villa to know she is eating and resting well. Pooja also told me there is not much progress regarding the meeting with the RC Group of companies, and Taani is still striving for the meeting. I want to do something for her to help her out. I have contacts here who work with the RC Group, and if I speak to them, they might help me put in a good word for Taani to help secure a meeting with them, at least. But I know doing so will again hurt her ego, and things might go further south in our relationship, which is not something I can afford at the moment.

On our fourth-month marriage anniversary a week ago, I had expected Taani to text me after receiving my cake and the gift through her sister, Vidhi, but even that didn't happen. On our wedding day, I saw Taani crying before her father's photo and wishing he was alive to see his daughters get married. That's when I decided to do something about her wish. Obviously, I couldn't bring her father back, but I could ensure his picture was included with our family photo. I knew some great graphic designers who could make it happen. When Taani showed me her old albums after marriage, I took the best picture of her father without her notice and gave it to my designer. But the final photo wasn't ready until days before I had to leave for London. And since Taani had fought with me that night, and I decided to fly to London immediately, I asked Vidhi to give this to Taani on our fourth month anniversary. I had prayed and hoped my wife would call me on that day at least, but by not even doing that, she broke my heart again. Was my relationship with her on the verge of breaking? No!!

"Sameer?" Dad's voice breaks my reverie. "You are sweating. What happened? Are you not feeling well?"

Dad touches my arm. We are in the car, and luckily Dad is driving us home today.

"I am fine, Dad. Just a bit tired."

"Of course you are. What's keeping your mind so busy? I have been noticing it for quite a few days. You are looking dull and depressed."

"I am missing my wife," I mention, which is true. I miss Taani a lot.

"Then go back to her or call her here. I know what it feels like to stay without your partner for even one night, so all I'll say is to finish the work sooner here and fly back to India. Taani must be missing you too."

I blankly nod. I just hope Taani is missing me too.

We reach home, and Mom looks ecstatic as she welcomes us.

"Hello, boys," she winks, surprising us.
"Wow, Meera. You sure are in a good mood."

Dad gives my mom a hug and a kiss on the forehead. And I am reminded of the time when I used to kiss Taani the same way when she would be back from work. Damn hell! I am jealous of my parents' romance, because I miss my good old days.

"I'll go freshen up. And Mom, I will have dinner early and rest. I am a bit tired."

"Sure, I will ask Taani to get the dinner table ready."

I nod and turn around, only to stop again. Taani? Did Mom say Taani?

"You said Taani?" I ask, turning back to Mom, who shakes her head in denial.
"No, I never said Taani. I said I will ask Mani to get the dinner ready."

Mani!! Mani is our butler. Even Dad looks surprised by Mom's answer as though he also heard her saying *'Taani'* and not *'Mani.'*

"Did you hear Taani?" Mom asks, and I am speechless. I did hear her saying Taani.
"He is missing her too much already, Meera," Dad smiles. "Don't tease him more. Go ahead, son. Freshen up, and we will see you at the dinner table."

I leave for my room, disheartened. It's been a routine now; I leave early for work, come home late and retire to my room only to keep tossing and turning on my bed, seeing Taani's pictures on my mobile, wishing she was here, with me.

I barge into my room, take off my tie, and throw it on the bed. Then I unbutton my shirt to take it off and throw it on the couch. I am about to unzip my trousers when I hear her voice.

"You were never this messy, Sameer."

Taani? I turn around and see her standing at the door. Am I hallucinating, or is she really here? I rub my tired eyes and once again look towards the door. And there she is, in a blue sleeveless dress hugging her curves and resting just above her knees. She's worn the dress I had gifted her before our marriage. She looks lovely, like a dream come true.

She lazily walks toward me while I stare at her, rooted to the spot. I can smell her perfume, and my heart is thumping inside my chest, telling me she is here for real.

"Hi," she smiles softly, looking into my eyes, standing two feet away from me.

It's confirmed. My wife is here in London, standing before me because even without touching her, I can feel her presence.

"What are you doing here, Taani?"

"I wanted to surprise you."

Surprise? I hope she isn't here to end things between us.

"Aren't you happy?" she asks, a bit nervous about my indifference.

I am shocked by her presence in London, and that too in my bedroom, a place where I have dreamed of making love to her in almost every corner. But then the bitter words she told me that night clouded my mind.

"The last time I recall, *you* weren't happy being around me," I state.

She looks guilty at my direct hit of words.

"Sameer, I-"

"Taani..." Dad rushes into our room, interrupting us. "Oh my god, you are really here? Meera just told me, and I couldn't stop myself from coming to meet you."

Taani quickly composes herself and touches my Dad's feet, who pulls her in for a hug.

"You gave us a lovely surprise, dear. Sameer was missing you like crazy."

Taani looks at me again, but I don't want her to see my pain. I only know what I went through, missing every little thing about her. No words can define my pain. Mom also enters the room, signalling Dad to leave us alone. Does she know something? From the looks Mom and Taani are giving each other, I get a fair idea that Mom is aware of why Taani is here and wants us to have some time alone, but I am unprepared for a confrontation. Not right now. Not like this.

"I'll take a shower and be right back," I tell them before turning away and heading straight to the bathroom. I need space for it to sink that my Taani is really here, with me, in my bedroom. And now that she is here, I am going to make sure we mend our relationship, and if not, I will keep on trying till I wear her out, and she has no choice but to accept me and our marriage.

I am overwhelmed that Taani took so much effort to fly here, probably leaving most of her work behind, only to meet me, which means she's as committed to making this work as I am. But her harsh words that night of making the biggest mistake of her life by marrying me still reverberate in my head every time I think about her. I don't think I can forget that anytime soon, not until Taani is clear about her priorities and my place in her life.

When I come downstairs, Taani is helping my Mom serve dinner. I realized she had already arranged her stuff in my room, in the closet, and at the bedside table, which meant she was staying here for a few days. As soon as I take the seat, Taani sits next to me and serves me. I won't stop her. She's my wife and has every right to do what she wants.

"You knew she was coming here?" I ask Mom, trying to sound neutral.

"No, she gave us all a big surprise, and we loved it, didn't we?" Mom chuckles.

I smile back at her and look at Taani, who is waiting for me to give her a reaction. I smile at her too, and she knows very well it is only because my parents are here.
"How's your work going?" I choose a safe topic as we begin eating.

"Good. How's yours?"
"Superb," I bite a morsel and suddenly choke on it.
"Sameer?" Taani quickly rubs my back, asking me to look up and hands me a glass of water to drink. Seeing her so worried for me makes me want her more. But maybe this is just an instinctive reaction to a person choking. Who knows? She would do that to anyone. I am not someone special. Though my heart negates that thought and assures me that I mean something more to my wife, my mind rebels.

Once I am fine, we resume eating.

"I think Sameer is unable to digest that you are here with him, Taani," Mom teases. "You have to do something special to make him believe it."
I cough again. What the hell is wrong with my table manners today? Either I am gobbling up the food in

a hurry or am forcing myself to eat even though my appetite is nonexistent.

"I think Sameer needs a dessert," Mom adds, pushing my favourite dessert, Suji halwa (Semolina pudding), towards me.

I take the first bite of the halwa, and I know it's not prepared by Mom but by Taani. In the last three months that we stayed together, this is the only dish Taani learnt to cook from me and for me. And I love it. I sneak a glance at Taani, who reddens as our eyes meet.
"The halwa is delicious," I praise with a soft smile. She looks up, surprised that I remembered the taste of her prepared dish and smiles back.

"Sameer, in that case, you should have some more." Mom serves me some more of it, and I happily eat it.

Dad and Mom continue discussing how they plan to show Taani around now that she is here and how she had planned her schedule back in Delhi so that her work doesn't suffer, while I keep eating my dessert quietly. Taani puts her palm over my thigh as she usually does when we sit together. My fingers itch to entwine with hers below the table, to raise our hands and kiss her fingers, or maybe use those supple fingers to do something else and relieve the ache that has been burning my body since the time we were distanced. But instead, I keep my cool and continue chatting with Dad. Neither have I shoved her hand away from my thigh nor have I given her any indication from my face or expressions that her gesture is creating havoc in my body.

I realize Taani keeps glancing at me as though unable to understand why I am acting so cold and not reacting to her touch, despite just praising her for the dessert, but I remain detached and continue eating.

Once the dinner is over, we retire to my bedroom, and like a good husband I am—and have always been—I check with her if she is comfortable with us sleeping on the same bed, or has a problem with that too.

"I can take the couch if you want," I say, alarming my wife.
"Couch? Why?"
"I am just guessing." I shrug. "I thought you might not like us sharing a bed anymore."
"If I didn't want to share your bed, I wouldn't be here in London in the first place, Sameer."

I stare at her blankly for a few seconds.
"Point noted," I say, nodding my head. I make my way to the bed, ignoring her completely.

"Sameer, I am sorry."

I stop for a second before continuing my way toward the bed. I arrange her pillows just the way she likes and continue to fix the duvet.

"Do you want one more comforter? The nights are cold here."

Seeing me disregard her apology, Taani continues.
"We need to talk, Sameer. I came all the way for you and to apologize to you."
"Should I close the curtains?" I ask, turning to the windows. "I think that should cozy up the room."

I close the windows and slide the curtains, but she continues to talk.

"I am not sleeping until you hear me out."
"Did you take your stress tablets?" I inquire and reach for her medicine pouch, which she has placed at the bedside table. That's when Taani loses her cool. She blocks my way and grabs my arms.

"Why do you even care whether I have my tablets or not if you want to ignore my apology?"
I don't reply, nor do I look at her. She pulls my chin up, forcing me to meet her eyes.

"I am sorry, Sameer. I shouldn't have said all that to you. I was... I was so annoyed that you made that decision for me the other day that..."
"And it will never change, Taani," I snap. "Even if God asks for your appointment and you are sick, I will not let him disturb you. That's because you are too precious to me."

She is astounded by my declaration.

"If this were to happen again, I am going to take the same decision, so don't bother to apologize if you are not willing to accept that in the future. Your health is my top priority. No business, yours or mine, and no amount of money, deals or projects is ever taking precedence over it. Remember that."

She swallows painfully as if processing my angry tirade.

"And that's not all, Taani. You disgraced our marriage. Why are you even here? Did Vansh's grandmother or anyone else cloud your mind again to fix things between us and have sent you here to mend our relationship? Is that why you left all your important work and flew here? If that's the case, I suggest you don't stay back for long. You apologized, and I forgive you. The matter is closed. Stop wasting your time convincing me only because others want you to do so."

"No… No, Sameer. No one sent me here. I came here because I wanted to mend things between us. I missed you."
Tears pool in her eyes.
"I missed you so badly that I couldn't stay in my own house, in my own room, only because you were not there with me. Our memories together in that house haunted me day and night, and I could literally see you and feel you in every corner of the house."

A tear rolls down her eye and I itch to wipe it off. It also pains me to realize I am the reason behind it. She missed me so much just as I did.

"I missed you too, Taani," I admit. "I spent sleepless nights because every word that came out of your mouth that night about your regret in marrying me stabbed my heart infinite times."

"I didn't mean it," she breaks down. "I didn't mean it, Sameer. Those words just slipped out of my mouth in anger."

"They did slip out because somewhere in your heart, you did think about it," I interrupt her. "You probably just married me because you had to get married at some point with someone, and I was the easy lay, isn't it?"

"No," she cries harder. "No, dammit. I married you because I felt a connection with you. Ever since I saw your picture when your proposal came for Vidhi, I felt a pull towards you, Sameer."

She cups my face while tears continue to roll down her cheeks.

"You brought out the woman in me that I was once. You made me feel like the real Taani and not the CEO Tanisha Gupta, which I am for the rest of the world. You kept showering your love on me and stole my heart every time you did something for me. The more I got to know you, the harder I started falling for you. I have never wanted or needed anyone else in my life before you, but after you, I cannot imagine my life without you. You will always be the only one I'll forever want."

I feel a sense of calm as she says this, but the pain is still there, and it won't go from my heart that easily. "I know I have hurt you badly, Sameer. And yet you kept giving me what I couldn't even imagine in my dreams. You know about my needs and my pain even before I admit them to myself. I am so ashamed of myself for hurting you, Sameer? I wish I hadn't said all that. How could I be so cruel? I am sorry... I am so sorry, Sameer. Please forgive me."

She presses her forehead with mine and continues to weep. I don't think I can see her in such a distressed state anymore, and I pull away to wipe her tears. "Stop crying."

She grips my wrists to let my palm touch her cheeks and holds it there as she continues to unburden herself.

"I wish I could love you the way you deserve, Sameer. I'm still learning. All these years after Dad's death, I have always been alone. There was no one whom I could make my priority, no one whom I could love enough. There was no one to teach me that true happiness and the essence of love lie in making your family your priority over everything else. I had no one to make me realize that, and soon, you came into my life. Maybe, I took you for granted, but not anymore. You mean the world to me, Sameer. No one else. Nothing else can come before you, I promise. Please forgive me. Please."

"I forgive you," I instantly reply. "But it's easier saying that than implementing, Taani. And, I don't want you to make me your priority. It's fine to focus on growing your business, but that should have nothing to do with our relationship. I accept it's my mistake too; I forgot to inform you about Pooja's call. Maybe if I had, you wouldn't have been so shocked, and we could have amended things together before it took a turn for the worse. So, I am guilty too, but by saying that you regret our marriage that day, you broke my heart, Taani."

She swallows her tears, nodding in agreement.
"It won't happen again."
I nod, accepting her words because I know she means it this time.
"You look exhausted, and after a long journey, you definitely need to sleep. Come here."

I try to drag her to the bed, but Taani stays rooted to the spot, and I know why. She wants me to carry her as I used to every time. Though my anger has mellowed down, and I feel a whole lot better knowing she loves me too and wants to make amends in our relationship for a happy future, this time, I'm going to take things slow. But the lover boy in me wants to fulfill Taani's unsaid wish. So, I lean down and carry Taani in my arms. The moment I do, she wraps her hands around my neck and allows me to take her to the bed. I lay her gently on her side of the bed and cover her up with the duvet. Turning the lights off, I take my side. I know Taani longs for me to erase this physical distance between us or give her some indication through my touch or words that I too seek the intimacy she craves, but when I don't give any heed to it, she rolls to my side of the bed and attempts to kiss me. I pull back away from her before our lips meet.

"We need to sleep, Taani."

It takes me an enormous amount of control to say this and move away from her, but it's the need of the hour. Whatever happened between us, I don't want us to take it lightly anymore and repeat it again. Taani frowns at me, and soon her face crumples, knowing I am avoiding intimacy. This time, she literally pleads.

"Can I just cuddle you, Sameer?"
Yes, I would like that. I want to believe my wife is here and we have just sorted out our differences, and from here onwards, it's only going to be happy times ahead. I pull her closer to me, and she instantly spoons me, burying her face in my chest and putting

her arms around my back so tight as if she is afraid to lose me again. That's my sweet Taani, my adorable wife. The one who doesn't want anything in the world except me. The urge to press our bodies closer drives me insane, but I control that urge and, instead, stroke her back, weaving my fingers in her hair to put her to sleep. For now, I just need both of us to give some time to accept and learn from what happened between us, making sure it never repeats ever again.

"I love you, Sameer. I love you so much," She keeps murmuring in her sleep. I am so touched by her declaration. Taani has never openly spoken these three words to me, and now hearing it from her mouth, in her voice, is no less than a blessing in itself. I cuddle her closer and softly kiss her hair, which she probably doesn't realize as she's fast asleep. I stare at my beautiful wife for a long time till sleep takes over.

CHAPTER 16

Taani

It's been three days since I arrived in London and stayed with Sameer. We have resolved all our differences, and though he behaves normally, takes care of me and goes shopping and sightseeing with me, he hasn't shown the urge to kiss me even on my forehead, forget kissing my lips or indulge in a make-out session. Why is he doing this? Why is he maintaining this distance when he says he has forgiven me? Every night we sleep, he lets me cuddle him and does nothing else. No grinding of bodies and no touching of lips on each other's skin, though he keeps stroking my head and patting my back to put me to sleep, as he would do to a child. I don't understand why he is so distant and his gestures so asexual?

From the time I'm here, Sameer has been working from home, which is great as I get to see him and be with him the entire day. Today morning when I woke up, he was getting dressed before the mirror and was totally oblivious to me ogling his hot body. And unlike before, he wears tight black briefs, not his regular boxers, which highlight the bulge inside, making me melt into a puddle. I literally had to squeeze my thighs and close my eyes to dampen the burning ache rising in my body. I don't know what Sameer wants to prove by ignoring me and seducing me, albeit unknowingly, at the same time.

Today, my patience is running out, so once Mom and Dad retire to their room for an afternoon nap, I barge into Sameer's room. He is working on his laptop but gives me a quick glance before turning his eyes back to his laptop screen.

"Why are you avoiding me, Sameer?" I ask openly. If he wants to fight, I am well prepared for it because until he tells me why he is doing this, I am not going to stop.

"Who told you I am avoiding you?" He asks without looking at me, busy typing away on his laptop.

"Then why are you not touching me?"

He pauses, and I notice his intense, hungry eyes. *On me!!*

"Come here," he demands.

Okay! I hadn't expected this. With baby steps, I reach Sameer, who keeps staring at me like I am his favourite dessert, which I obviously am, and giving me a once-over from head to toe. I am wearing a short blue bodycon dress, revealing my long legs. The moment I reach his chair behind the cozy workspace that Sameer has set up in his room, he stretches his hand, and I instantly shut my eyes, anticipating his next move. He pokes his finger on my arm.

"I touched you. Happy?"
My eyes open in shock. Really? That's it? Just a poke of his finger on my arm? Sameer is definitely teasing me on purpose, making me feel all edgy, while he continues to type again on the laptop.

"That's not what I meant by touch," I groan.
"No? Then what did you mean?"
I bite my lip in nervousness, and gathering courage, ask Sameer what I want from him.
"I want to sit on your lap."
"My legs are hurting," he lies and gets up from the chair, turning away from me.

His legs are hurting? Seriously?

"Sameer, this is not done."
I follow him to the bedside table, where he goes to get his phone. Just then, my mobile rings aloud beside his phone. Sameer takes it and passes it to me.
"It's Pooja," he says.
I cross my arms at the front without taking the phone, surprising him.
"Taani, take your mobile and answer the call."
"I don't want to."
"What?"

He looks shocked. I sit at the edge of the bed as I know he is going to hound me to answer the phone call.
"Taani, Pooja might have some important business matters to discuss. That's why she is calling

you. Pick her call, dammit. What the hell is wrong with you?"

"Nothing is wrong, Sameer. I just don't feel like picking up any calls, and I don't want to do any business either. I don't care what emergency they might have there."

I blow on my recently manicured nails lazily. Sameer cusses something before answering the call himself.

"Yes, Pooja. What is it?"

I can read Sameer like a book; he is totally pissed off and unsettled because I am doing something he never expected me to do, ever.

"Yeah, she is around but is not willing to answer the call. I'm putting you on speaker. Just talk to her," Sameer adds, pressing the speaker button.

"Pooja," I shout. "Please ask the board members to appoint another CEO to take over the helm of the Gupta Industries."

My remark shocks both Sameer and Pooja.

"Ma'am?" Pooja stutters.

"What the hell are you saying?" Sameer barks at me.

"I am quitting. I don't want to run any business. My husband is my only priority from now on," I reply, snatching my phone from him and turning off the speaker mode. "Pooja, just do as I said."

Sameer grabs the phone from me, completely losing his cool.

"Pooja, don't listen to her orders. Just stay put, okay. I think your Ma'am has lost her mind after coming to London. I'll put some sense into her, and she will call you back."

He disconnects the call and turns toward me.

"Are you kidding me, Taani? That's your father's company you are talking about, and you want to resign?"

"Yes, I want to resign because I want to be your wife first. Nothing else matters to me anymore."

Sameer rakes his fingers in his hair, annoyed.

I get up from the bed to reach him. I cup his face, stroking his French beard, and Sameer calms down.

"What other proof do you want, Sameer, to believe that I am not the Taani you left behind in India? I even confessed to you the first night I came here that I...."

I pause when his dark gaze returns to me and stays glued to my face.

"What confession?" He darkly inquires.

I know I have to bite my attitude and ego and lay myself bare before Sameer. He knows I was murmuring those three magical words to him that night. Yet, he wants me to say them again. Fine. If saying those words makes him forgive me and accept me as his wife in the true sense, then I am ready.

"I love you, Sameer." There! I say it.

Sameer swallows and his Adam's apple bobs up and down, luring my attention to his neck.

"I couldn't hear you well," he mocks. "What did you say?"

Oh damn! This man is going to kill me with his arrogance. I move closer to him, touch our lower bodies lightly, and repeat.

"I love you, Sameer."

"Loudly, Taani. I didn't hear it well enough."

"I love you...," I say loud enough for even his parents to hear in the other room. And I don't stop. "I love you. I love you. I love you, Sameer Khanna. I love you."

I would have kept going with my confession, but Sameer put his palm over my mouth to shut me up.

"Okay, okay. Shh... I heard. Alright? I heard." He takes a deep breath, and I see his lips tilt in a smile. Yes, definitely a smile.

But soon, it disappears. I want to know what is going on in Sameer's mind at the moment, but he just leaves me and walks out of the room.

"Sameer?" I call behind him, but he doesn't wait. What the hell!

****

By the next day, I was totally annoyed. Sameer is not at home today but has been working from his office, so I can't even spend time with him or see him until he is back. I never thought that it would take me days to woo back the very man who fell for me instantly, at first look. Forget days; I think it will take me ages to charm him again and make him believe he is all I want and nothing else.

"Taani?" Mom enters the kitchen. "What happened? Why are you banging the vessels so loudly?"

"I am just taking out my frustration on them, Mom, as I can't take it out on your dear son."

She laughs at my remark.

"What did Sameer do now? I thought everything was well between you two after you apologized to him, and especially after yesterday when you screamed about your love for him for the whole house to hear."

"I did, yeah," I shrug, embarrassed that everyone heard.

"Then, what happened?

"Then, nothing. That's what, Mom. Nothing happened," I whine. "I confessed my love for him and that I wanted him above and beyond my ambitions, my company and yet, he is throwing his attitude around. Sameer told me that he forgave me, but I don't think he really did. Can you believe it? He hasn't even kissed me yet since I came to London."

I shut my mouth, mortified for blurting that to my mother-in-law, who bursts into laughter.

"Aww, Taani. I know my son. He is just playing with you, teasing you. Maybe in some corner of his heart, he is still hurt and will need time to introspect his feelings, but you don't stop chasing him. You are his wife and a beautiful one at that. Every wife has her unique methods to get her husband's attention."

The way she explains it to me, a naughty idea begins to form in my head. Before I can think about how to proceed with my idea, Mom reaches me and cups my face.

"I will take your father-in-law out for dinner and also give the staff a night off. So, when Sameer returns home tonight, you can implement whatever plan you have up your sleeve to get his attention and be sure to win his heart this time."

I grin. Mom is right. I have to take matters into my own hands if I want my husband back. He is hurt, I agree, and I hurt him, which is why I am going to win him back tonight, ease all his pains and put all his suspicions and worries to rest. I am going to give him his wife, Taani, the one he is yearning for.

In the evening, when I am all set with the plan and so is my mother-in-law, Sameer's Dad has his own tantrums.

"Meera, c'mon. How can we plan a private dinner leaving Taani all alone at home? Even Sameer is going to be late tonight. Besides, I want to spend some time with my daughter-in-law. She is always busy with Sameer and you. I never get time with her to even talk about how her business is going on. I am sorry, cancel the plan. We'll go some other day."
Seeing dad's resolve of not wanting to go shocks both; Mom and me.
"Sandeep," Mom sits next to Dad. "You are not getting my point. Taani won't be alone for long. Sameer will be home in an hour."
"Then let him come home, and we can all go for dinner together."

Oh, God! How can we convince Dad that the plans I have with Sameer tonight cannot be implemented until we are home alone?

"Sandeep, enough of your drama," Mom fakes some anger. "You are not interested in having romantic dinners with me alone anymore. Like father, like son."
Mom is subtly signalling to him about leaving us alone, but when Dad is still ignorant, I step in.

"Dad, I'll be fine alone," I say. "In fact, I am planning to give a small surprise to Sameer when he returns."

I blush when I recall what the surprise is, and I hope Sameer likes it too.

"Oh, what is the surprise?" Dad innocently queries, and now I want to run away. I can't tell him that. "Sandeep," Mom pulls him from the couch. "Let the kids handle the surprise without telling us the details. You and I are going out. Don't wreck Taani's plans. Please."

Finally, Dad understands that I want to be alone with Sameer, so Mom has been insisting they go out.

"Sure... sure. Why didn't you two tell me this beforehand? I don't want to spoil my kids' fun. Meera, c'mon. Let's go. I am taking you to your favourite restaurant for dinner tonight and then maybe we will stay back the night at the same hotel. It's been a long time since we had some private time too."

Mom pats his arms, hiding her blush.

"Now he is talking." She winks at me. "Taani, sweetheart, all the best, and see you and Sameer tomorrow morning. Good night."
"Good night." I wave at them and lock the door.

Now that I am all alone, I have time to get ready. Sameer has his own set of keys to enter the house, and he is going to get a huge surprise after that.

Sameer

Taani's consistent efforts to get my attention ever since she returned to me still bring a smile to my face. Her confession that she loves me and wants to make me her only priority from now on has given me a renewed vigour in almost everything I do. No, I don't want her to resign from the company or ignore her other responsibilities for me, but I am still thrilled to know she even thought about that, which proves how much I and our relationship matter to her. I have forgiven her. Of course, I have, but I can't forget all those hurtful things she said to me earlier as they truly broke my heart. But eventually, I will overcome all that and give Taani her husband back, the man I was when we were together in India. A husband who is still completely smitten by her charm, her intelligence, her resolve to set things right, and so much more. But not so soon. I want to see to what lengths Taani can go to persuade me. I love Taani as a whole, with her goodness and flaws, and I want them both; there is no doubt about that.

I enter the house with my set of keys after returning from work. It looks like there is no one at home. My parents had messaged me saying they were going out for dinner, but where was the other staff? And Taani? Is she out too? The house is in darkness, and I switch on the lights, but they don't work. What the heck! What happened to the electricity? I switch on my phone torchlight and make my way to the stairs, and that's when I see the pathway of rose petals decorated from the base of the stairs all the way up. Hold on. Who did this? I keep climbing the stairs, and the rosy path leads me to my bedroom. Definitely, this is one of Taani's attempts to surprise and tempt me. Well, I am stunned, to be honest. I am aware doing all this must have taken time and effort.

As soon as I push the door open, the sweet fragrance of the scented lavender candles fills my nostrils. A soft romantic melody plays in the background. Though the room is dark, there is enough light for me to see the gorgeous woman, my wife Taani, wearing only a blue negligee in the name of clothes to cover her private parts, lying seductively on the bed, which is again decorated by more rose petals. What... the... F*ck... I throw my laptop bag on the recliner. Drawn like a moth to a flame, I rush towards Taani, who squirms on the bed with a winning smile that finally, she did manage to get all my attention. I am seeing her like this after such a long time, desperate for my touch, craving for me. I hungrily roam my eyes over every curve of her body, pausing for a moment more on her heaving breasts which I love the most, and reach the bed. I would be a fool of a man to miss this opportunity to devour his wife, who is on his bed like a sinful temptation, spread out only for him to touch and claim.

To say I'm pleasantly shocked is still an understatement. My arousal twitches in anticipation as I reach the bed. Taani stretches her milky white arm for me, and I hold her hand, dipping the edge of the bed with my knee. She kisses my fingers before moving them on her face and unties the knot of my tie, taking it out in no time.

We stare at each other; my heart does a happy dance in my chest as she draws me closer and closer, making me lean on her face completely so she can lock our lips.

Just then, realization dawns on me, and I quickly pull myself away.

"Sameer?" Taani's hurt voice breaks me too, but without giving her another look, I make my way to the walk-in closet of my room. Taking off my shirt, I shove it in the laundry basket before opening the closet door to find my nightwear. As I am about to pick a t-shirt, Taani creeps up behind me and wraps her arms around my waist, pressing her cheeks on my naked back.

"I don't know what else to do, Sameer, to get my husband back. I am not very good at this. Without you, my confidence in mending our relationship is wavering. I have tried everything. From having left my work, to focusing on being a good wife to you and a good daughter-in-law, I am trying it all. If you think a baby can help fix our marriage and make you believe in my sincerity towards our relationship, I am even ready for that. I am ready to have your baby. I-"

Her voice is thick with tears, but she pauses abruptly, and that's when I feel the wetness of her tears on my back. She is crying. Damn hell! I instantly turn around and pull her in my arms.

"Taani, stop crying," I kiss her tears away.

She looks overwhelmed that I kissed her tears.

"Whoever gave you the idea that a baby can fix a couple's relationship is completely wrong. Get it out of your head. A baby at this stage, where a couple is still figuring out their roles and responsibilities of married life, can worsen things."

"What else was I supposed to do, Sameer? You were not even looking at me. I was afraid that you were withdrawing yourself from me. I don't want to lose you."

"I don't want to lose you either. And no, I am not withdrawing myself from you or this relationship. I love you, Taani. But the things you told me have hurt me. Yes, I have forgiven you, but I need some time to forget those words. And most importantly, you gave me a hard time when I chased you, so I thought you should get a taste of your own medicine too, by wooing me back."

"I have tasted that medicine enough," she mutters. "And I mean it, Sameer. If you still play this ignorant game with me, I will give up my life."

That's it. I am so angry at her for saying that; I give her a hard, punishing kiss, nipping her lower lip instead of sucking it as she likes. Taani scoops me in her arms, sliding her hands around my neck and trying to deepen the kiss and that's when I pull away.

"Never say that again," I scowl.

She nods her head and gives me a forlorn look as though she is unsure what I will do next. I feel like a heel for making her upset and making her yearn for me. My wife was on the verge of doing anything and everything to get me back. How can my anger not melt on seeing my bold and wild Taani turn into a soft kitten? I am not a man who can hold grudges for long.

Taani's gaze lingers hungrily on my bare chest as though contemplating if touching me will make me withdraw again. I pull her chin up. A fire begins to burn inside me on seeing her in my favourite colour lingerie, barely covering her from my eyes. It's a garment made for seduction, and I wonder when Taani bought one for herself?

"I have missed this," Taani whispers, grazing her fingers on my French beard. "The feel of it on my cheeks… neck… and lower…."

The moment she says this, I push her with my body against the closet. We both gasp together at the sudden shift of the positions.

"I'm starving for you, Taani."

"That's why I am here," she replies. "To let you feast on me."

F*ck! My control is on edge after her naughty words. I tilt her face towards me and give her another hard kiss, taking my own sweet time to feast on her lips and play with her tongue. I have held her so tight that there's no room for even air to pass in between us. I am achingly aware she is dripping wet for me, and that's when I decide to give each other the relief that we have been craving for so long. We surely deserve it.

Sliding the door of the walk-in closet open, I push all the clothes away, almost throwing them on the floor to make some space for my wife. She knows what is coming when I grip her waist and make her sit on one of the freed sections inside the closet, and she instantly wraps her legs around my waist. With our faces so close, my desperate fingers tear off the satin fabric into two, letting it fall, baring her upper body for me to ravish. I look at her gorgeous full breasts, eyeing them hungrily and look back into her eyes.

"I can't be easy on you tonight after starving for weeks without you, Taani. So, don't expect me to go slow."

"I don't want slow," she groans, stroking my face with her palms.

"You are playing with fire."

"I want to burn in that fire."

"Your wish is my command" I grunt. "Then let's burn together."

My patience runs out, and I let my hands roam over her silky skin before slipping my fingers inside the thin straps of her lacy undergarment and tearing them off. Shedding my own trousers and briefs aside, I am ready to rock our night and the coming ones. Before she can predict my next move, I kiss her stomach and leave a trail of kisses downwards till I reach her aching wetness and taste her sensitive folds, lapping her up like a starved man, until she shudders in my arms. I had missed her taste on my lips and her moans, a sign of her pleasure. Just when she is about to find a release, I rise back on my feet and enter her without any warning. Taani lets out a surprised cry. Oh, God, she feels like home, and it's great to come home after staying away for so long. With our bodies moving rhythmically, I slam inside her like a fire waiting to erupt. It's been too long. She closes her eyes, but her hands keep exploring my body, every inch of it. She's in pain, and so am I. Taani keeps tugging my hair and moaning my name while I keep nipping her creamy white skin, fondling her ample breasts and pinching her taut buds while our lower bodies are talking their own language, in sync with each other, faster and harder until we give us the relief, we have been holding inside us for long. I then give her a lingering kiss after having emptied ourselves of our desires. I kiss her to thank her for considering me worthy enough to be chased by her. I then carry her to the bed, promising not to end this moment until we are exhausted and can't even think of getting down from the bed for the next few days. Yep, that's my plan, and I will implement it.

"Did you send Mom and Dad out tonight?" I ask, pushing myself inside her again, when we are on the bed, Taani lying underneath me like a goddess.

"Yes…" she cries. "Mom's idea but … I… I knew it would be worth it."

I let out a grunt as she confessed and bit her shoulder.

"You little minx, this is the best day of my life."

"Mine too." Taani kisses me hard.

She's on a mission tonight to exhaust my mind and body. I have never been this rough with her before during our lovemaking as I am tonight. And the best part is, she loves every bit of it.

"It's been a long time since I feel so good again, Sameer,"

"Me too. It's been too damn long."

"Focus." She mentions as I slip out of her accidentally. It's not my fault. She's dripping with my love.

I get inside her again, bend down and capture her lips. It takes a few more thrusts, and we are in heaven, fully satiated and contended with each other. After multiple rounds of lovemaking, we both are spent, and I scoop Taani in my arms and cuddle her.

She is already sleepy, and I am still hard for her—still insatiable.
"In a week, we can fly back to India," I mention kissing her forehead. "I am finished with most of the work here."

Taani looks up at me with dreamy eyes.
"I can continue the rest of my work from India, don't worry," I assure her.
"I know, but so can I," she smiles.
"How?"

"Before I flew to London, Vidhi told me about her wish that she is ready to join me as a business partner to divide the work. You know I had offered her this role when she came to India, but she had refused it then, as she didn't have working experience. But now Vidhi thinks she has gained enough experience to take up this challenging role. Moreover, Vansh and I are always there to support her if needed. So, with Vidhi managing the business in India, I can be here with you in London and work from here. You don't have to sacrifice all the time, Sameer. I can too because this is what I want. We love each other equally, so we will divide our sacrifices equally too."

I like how she thinks and I kiss her nose and hug her close to my body.

"So, we'll do it this way," I continue. "Six months we will stay in India, where you will focus on your business, and the rest of six months we will stay in London where I can focus on mine. How does that sound?"

"Great. Mom and Dad can toggle with us if they like or can come to meet us anytime they want to."

"Done."

"I am not done with you yet," she pouts, kissing my chest and then her lips trail lower, exactly where I want her to. Damn hell! And while she works her mouth down, I shut my eyes in contentment as I sigh in relief. Taani is at last mine, body and soul. Finally, our love story, which began by chance, is complete.

EPILOGUE

Taani

SEVEN MONTHS LATER

My life is blooming like the yellow tulips that Sameer always gives me on our monthly marriage anniversaries. But today, the flowers are extra special since they convey his pride and his best wishes. Yes, we have done it. Gupta Industries has bagged the deal with the RC Group of Companies, a dream that I carried for years. I relentlessly chased that, and with Vidhi by my side and Sameer's guidance and support, I offered the company a deal they couldn't refuse.

I kiss the bouquet of the yellow tulips Sameer gave me today and keep it on the bedside table. I take a good look at myself in the mirror, making sure I look good for tonight's party that the RC Group have especially thrown for the business venture that they are collaborating with my company. I can't wait to be a part of that event. Vidhi is coming with Vansh, and my other close friend, Rohan, is also coming as he has recently taken over one of the subsidiaries of the

RC Group—their Jewellery brand that has multiple stores across the country and abroad. Rohan has expanded his father's business, bringing it to new heights, with the RC Group Jewellery division, his latest acquisition.

My life is perfect now. Sameer has filled my life with a riot of colours of love and passion. He still continues to fulfill my long list of pending desires which I couldn't previously since my work consumed me. We travel a lot. He still loves cooking for me, and thankfully I know how to cook a lot more than just Suji halwa (semolina pudding). Mom and Dad always make it a point to attend important events of our lives, like our birthdays and a party like tonight for which they have travelled from London to congratulate me and be a part of my happiness.

"Sameer? We are getting late. C'mon."

I adjust the plunging neckline of my silver dress, exposing a hint of my cleavage. This was again Sameer's gift to me. He is always shopping for me wherever he goes, and I love that he knows my choice so well. First, he buys me these beautiful outfits and then when I wear them, he is always in a hurry to get me out of them so he can ravage me.

"I'm ready," Sameer reaches behind me and takes a look at himself in the dressing mirror. My husband looks dishy enough to be devoured. In a grey three-piece suit, with his French beard neatly trimmed, hair spiked at the front and cut short at the back, Sameer is drop-dead gorgeous tonight. When I keep ogling at his mirror reflection, Sameer catches my eye and grins.

His eyes soon linger on my dress, from the platinum chain he gave me on our six-month marriage anniversary to the hint of cleavage visible, and move further down to my curves highlighted by the figure-hugging dress. In a fraction of a second, he closes the gap between our bodies, rubbing his lower body against mine, revealing how much turned on he is at the moment and kisses me on the nape of my neck.

"You look ravishing," he murmurs, placing another feathery kiss on that same spot. "Do we have a few minutes for a quickie?"

"No." I giggle, turning around and fixing his tie. "We are already late. Besides, Mom and Dad are ready and waiting for us downstairs."

"Alright. I'll get you out of this dress tonight when we are back home and will have my way with you."

"With pleasure." I wink at him while he kisses my forehead.

"I am so proud of you, Taani. We all are. Even your accomplishments are such a turn-on."

"Gosh, Sameer. Turn off the lover boy in you for the moment, or else I will not be able to hold my blush throughout the event. And, remember, I could only achieve this because I have your undying support. We both have spent sleepless nights on this deal. While I was working late nights on my laptop, you were watching over me and waiting for me to return to you. So, we are both equally responsible for winning this prestigious project."

He doesn't argue and tucks a strand of my hair behind the ear.

"I'm always there for you, Taani."

"I know, and I feel blessed."

I hug him tight and look lovingly at our wedding photo frame hung on the wall behind; the one Sameer got photoshopped by adding my father's picture. I was so alone after Dad, but Sameer and his family have shaped my life again, and I can't thank the almighty enough for showering this blessing on me.

Sameer

The party is in full swing. Vansh and I share a drink together, keeping an eye on our wives, Vidhi and Taani, respectively, and hearing praises about their achievements.

"They look jubilant tonight," Vansh mentions, taking a swig of his drink.

"Yeah, I haven't seen Taani this happy in a long time," I answer.

"Exactly. You have changed her for good. She lived a hollow life previously, despite having friends like Rohan and me."

"She needed love," I mention, admiring my wife, who looks like a goddess tonight.

"Indeed."

"Who needed love?" Rohan Oberoi swings his arms around our shoulders.

"There he comes," I grin, turning around and hugging Rohan. Vansh and Rohan do the same after I pull back.

Rohan orders a drink for himself and takes a seat next to us.

"You are late. Where were you?" I ask Rohan.

"I had to pick up my car from the service station."

"But I didn't kick your car again. Why was it sent for servicing?" Vidhi teases as she and Taani join our group.

They finally found the time for us, not that I am complaining. Taani and Vidhi deserved to bask in their success tonight and meet new people in their business circle.

Vidhi and Rohan still bicker every time they meet, and their cute bantering keeps us entertained. Tonight, they are at it again.

"Do you know, Vansh?" Rohan turns to Vansh. "The number of times your wife has ruined my cars by her constant kicking, I think I should shut my jewellery business and open a garage instead. Oberoi Car Service Centre. She can bring me a lot of newer clients."

"Oh, please, I only kick your cars because you and your silly ideas mess with my head, Rohan."

"Oh, yeah?" Rohan laughs. "Don't forget whenever you and Vansh get into a fight; I am the one you take ideas from to patch up."

"And they don't work."

"Hell, they don't. You liar."

"Alright, alright. Just stop both of you." Taani intervenes, sliding her arm around my waist as we stand closer. "You both need a break."

"In fact, we all need a break," I suggest. "How about a vacation?"

Rohan raises his glass to toast.

"I am in, guys, but after a month. As you all know, I have just taken over the RC Group's jewellery stores, and the seamless transition will take time. In fact, I am flying to Mumbai tomorrow and will be busy with work for a few weeks."

"We are in no hurry, Rohan. As it is, we don't miss you so much." Vidhi teases.

"I don't miss you either, Dumbo," Rohan mocks her back, but pulls Vidhi to him for a hug when she pouts.

Rohan might be Vansh's friend, but he's always been a brotherly figure for Vidhi, and they do have heart-to-heart conversations also, apart from their bickering, which is, as I said, entertaining. Not to mention, Vidhi is very protective of Rohan as she knows the hurt and heartbreak he's gone through in the past.

"The whole gang is here," Mr. Anant Chopra, the 68-year-old CEO of the RC group of companies, interrupts us.

We happily greet him and wish him luck for his upcoming venture with Gupta Industries. He also talks about Rohan's acquisition of his jewellery business and mentions he was glad to have found a worthy buyer like Rohan.

"You'll love our exclusive jewellery line, Rohan, since they are designed by our best in-house designer. And hold on, here she comes. Let me proudly introduce you all to her."

We all turn around as he points out a woman walking towards us in a wine-coloured asymmetrical floor-length gown. She looks stunning. But as soon as she nears us, her smile wavers as her eyes meet with Rohan. They both look at each other in shock. Do they know each other?

Definitely, yes! The way Rohan has his glass in a tight grip says it all.

"Ladies and Gentlemen, meet Ishika Bhatia, the lead jewellery designer of my company," Anant Chopra introduces us.

Taani and Vansh glance at each other before turning to Rohan, who suddenly freezes. It looked like Vansh and Taani also knew Ishika just like Rohan does. Interesting!

"Hello, Rohan," Ishika stretches her hand for a formal handshake with him. He takes a few seconds to process what is happening before taking her hand.

"Hi, Ishika." His voice is barely a whisper.

"Long time," she adds.

"Yeah. Long time." Rohan nods in agreement while their hands are still linked.

Wow! What is that?

We greet each other and share pleasantries, after which, Anant Chopra takes his lead jewellery designer away. As soon as they leave, Rohan puts the glass away, almost shivering in anger and excuses us on the pretext of making a call.

"So, she is the Ishika you told me about?" Vidhi asks Vansh, who nods in affirmation and rubs his forehead, curbing his own surprise over the situation. Vansh assures Taani and Vidhi that he will follow Rohan and check on him. I am the only one confused and speechless over this entire scenario.

When I ask Taani about Ishika once we are alone, she sighs in disappointment.

"That's another complicated story to tell, Sameer. But yes, I think it's going to be a challenging time for Rohan in the coming days."

Oh damn! I knew it. Behind the mask of that mischievous all-is-well persona was a man whose heart was deeply hurt and looked like Ishika Bhatia had something to do with it.

"Hey," Taani pulls me to her. "Dance?"

My smile is back. She leans to my ear next.

"And don't worry, this time neither will I stamp your feet nor your heart, Mr. Sameer Khanna."

"I trust you on that, Mrs. Taani Khanna," I reply with a naughty smirk.

She leads me to the dance floor. The sound of music floats in the air as we groove in sync, in each other's embrace, completely smitten by the other and madly in love. With my wife, Taani, in my arms, my little world is complete. When I tell her that, she gives me her beautiful smile tempting me to lean in and kiss her softly. It's perfect. Just like our life together is.

THE END

Thanks for reading '**Love By Chance**' Please don't forget to rate and review the same in Amazon. Your ratings and reviews matter to me.

If you haven't read the Hidden Marriage Romance of Vansh Kapoor and Vidhi Gupta, you can read it in my book '**Mr & Mrs Kapoor' (Book 3 of Mr & Mrs Series)**

Also don't forget to check my Instagram Account **@madhuritamse** to get the updates on my next releases.

Get in touch with me at any of the below:

Blogs: https://madhuswritingden.wordpress.com/
Twitter: @Madhuri0302
Instagram: @Madhuritamse

MY OTHER BOOKS ON AMAZON

Below Books are available in Amazon Kindle.

Scan the below Code and Click on the Amazon Link that pops up on your phone.